For my Mum.

For your ability to stop complete strangers

on trains and tell them to read my books.

CHAPTER ONE

Smith shivered on the bench in his back garden. He lit his second cigarette of the day, put it in his mouth and left it there. He wrapped both hands around the coffee cup, but the coffee was already cold. It was early December and a sudden cold front had swept in from the Arctic and now the weather forecasters were confident in their predictions that an icy spell would mean sub-zero temperatures for the whole of Scotland and northern England for the next week.

The cigarette in Smith's mouth had gone out so he gave in, spat it out and went back inside. He closed the back door behind him, boiled the kettle for another cup of coffee, and sat down at the table. A sudden twinge in his right leg made him wince. The sudden stabs of pain were becoming more and more frequent. After his leg was broken in a rather unorthodox skydiving landing a few months earlier Smith's doctors had warned that there was the possibility of it happening, especially in colder weather. Smith's wrist had also been fractured, but so far he hadn't experienced any more pain from the break.

DC Erica Whitton came in. Her hair was soaking wet from the shower. "Where's the boss?" Smith asked, stood up and kissed his wife on the lips. "She's still asleep," Whitton told him. "I think she feels like a lie-in." ""I don't blame her. The weather is Baltic out there. How come you're up? I thought you had a couple of days off."

"I do, but I'm not like you. I can't just lie in bed all day."

"What? The only time I lie in bed all day is when I'm straight-jacketed to a hospital bed."

"They're going to send you a Christmas card this year."

"Excuse me?"

"The hospital. You've been a regular guest there this year."

It was true – Smith hadn't added up exactly how long he'd spent in hospital in the past year, but it probably equated to roughly a quarter of the year.

He was about to say something witty when his mobile phone started to ring on the table in front of him. He looked at the screen and saw it was a number not in his address book.

"Smith?" he answered.

The line was quiet on the other end. Smith had experienced calls like this plenty of times before – there always seemed to be people out there who got a kick out of nuisance calls. He was about to reject the call when he heard a faint voice on the other end.

"I want to live."

That was what Smith thought he'd heard. "I want to live."

"Who is this?" Smith asked but that was as far as the conversation went. He ended the call and got up to make coffee.

"Who was that?" Whitton asked.

"Prank call by the sound of it," Smith replied. "Somebody with nothing better to do."

"What time do you have to be at the station?"

"Nine. Brownhill has decided the brief about the illegal fireworks isn't exactly life or death and doesn't warrant a stupid-o'clock meeting."

"It's been quiet for the past few weeks," Whitton said.

"Too quiet. Superintendent Smyth is positively drooling with glee. It's quite a disturbing sight. His crime stats presentation is coming up next month. I almost wish we'd get a spate of juicy murders before then just to wipe the inane grin off his face."

Whitton laughed. "Don't say things like that. You should know by now, you ought to be careful what you wish for. I'll go up and check on Laura."

A few minutes later, Whitton walked back in with a small child in tow. Laura Smith was almost two now, and she'd inherited the stubbornness shared by both her parents, and, since she'd now realised what her feet could do, she'd insisted that being carried was for babies.

"She's growing up so fast," Smith bent down and kissed his daughter on the top of her head.

He left his head there for a while and breathed in the scent of her.

"Stop sniffing her," Whitton said. "You're worse than the dogs."

"Speaking of dogs, where are the two hooligans?"

The hooligans in question were Theakston, a Bull Terrier and Fred, the toad-like Pug.

"Still asleep," Whitton replied. "They don't like the cold."

"Who does?" Smith drained what was left in his coffee cup. "I'd better be off. Enjoy the day off. I'd curl up in front of the fire if I were you – this weather's only going to get worse according to the experts."

Smith arrived at the station twenty minutes later. A thin layer of ice had formed on the roads and he had to drive slowly the whole way. He got out of the car, rubbed his hands and quickly made his way inside. DS Bridge and DC Yang Chu were obviously sharing a joke by the front desk. Bridge was roaring with laughter. Smith watched as he patted Yang Chu on the shoulder.

Smith walked over to them. "What's so funny?"

"You tell him," Bridge said to Yang Chu.

"It seems Old Smyth has a hidden talent," Yang Chu said.

"I very much doubt that," Smith said. "And it's Superintendent Smyth to you."

"I was having a few drinks yesterday at a new place that's opened in town," Yang Chu carried on. "On Sunday afternoons they have a karaoke hour. Not my thing – idiots making fools out of themselves."

"One of those idiots was Superintendent Smyth," Bridge added.

Smith found himself smiling. "You're kidding. What song did he massacre?"

"Some Michael Bolton crap," Yang Chu told him. "And the worst part is he wasn't half bad. He got really into it. I almost didn't recognise him."

"So, what's so funny?"

"His voice is OK, but it's his dancing that had the whole room in stitches." Yang Chu went on to demonstrate. It was like something out of the seventies – Saturday Night Fever stuff.

"I wish I'd had my phone on me," he said when he'd finished. "It was totally surreal seeing old Smyth dance like that."

"Don't look now," Bridge warned. "John Travolta just walked in."

Superintendent Jeremy Smyth closed the door behind him, removed his scarf and gloves and walked over to them. Smith was finding it hard to keep a straight face. Bridge and Yang Chu were also struggling to compose themselves.

"Good morning," Smyth addressed all three of them. "Rather cold today wouldn't you say."

"Yes, sir," Yang Chu replied.

"So, what particular war are we fighting at the moment?" Smyth asked.

"Just trying to stay alive, sir," Smith said with a serious expression on his face. "That's what it's all about isn't it? Staying alive?"

Bridge started to chuckle. Yang Chu kept his lips tightly together, and his eyes were bulging.

Smyth looked at them, obviously perplexed. "Very good."

He marched off towards his office. He didn't even turn around when the guffaws of laughter exploded behind him.

CHAPTER TWO

One hour earlier

The mail landed on the carpet inside the door at 8:30 on the dot, as it always did during the week. Frank Broadbent, sleepy-eyed and slightly hungover from the night before scooped it up and took it with him to the kitchen. He dumped it on the table without bothering to see what had arrived. He made the strongest cup of coffee he could handle and lit a cigarette. The first drag always made him feel slightly nauseous but after the second or third his headache was starting to fade and the rush from the nicotine spread throughout his body and made him feel slightly better. Frank wasn't due at work until noon, but the thought of it made his headache even worse. He was the manager of a chain-run family restaurant and bar. An empty pub on a Monday in early December. He knew exactly what that meant – replenishing stock and putting together Christmas menus. For a second, Frank thought about phoning in sick but dismissed the thought as soon as it had appeared in his head. In two years, he had never phoned in sick and he'd never been late. He sipped the coffee and turned his attention to the pile of mail on the table. He leafed through it and sighed – there was what looked like a final reminder from a mail-order catalogue he'd foolishly subscribed to, tempted by the initial free offers. He didn't even need to open the letter to know he owed them precisely one hundred and eighty five pounds. He tossed the reminder aside and picked up the next one – another final reminder, this time from the gas company. Frank groaned. It was December - the cold weather had gripped the country and now his gas was about to be cut off. He could boil the kettle for a warm bath, but he had no idea how he was going to stay warm without the central heating. Most of the other correspondence was junk mail and he didn't even bother to open it.

The padded envelope was at the bottom of the pile. It was an A4 size white envelope. Frank's name and address was handwritten neatly in black-block capitals. Frank turned the envelope over and saw there was no indication of where it came from. No company stamp, no return address. Nothing. He was intrigued. An instruction to 'OPEN HERE' was written in the same hand as the address at the top. Frank wasted no time. He ripped open the top of the envelope and felt something prick his right index finger just above the knuckle.

"What the hell?" he exclaimed.

He dropped the envelope and looked at his finger. A single drop of blood appeared. It wasn't painful – it was more of a shock than anything else. Frank wiped away the blood and frowned. He wasn't sure what had just happened. Frank had worked for the Post Office for fifteen years before he left to manage the restaurant – he was used to paper cuts, but he knew straight away this wasn't a paper cut.

He took a knife from the drawer and carefully picked up the envelope. He held it at the bottom and slid the knife inside.

His mouth suddenly felt incredibly dry, and when he licked his lips, he was sure he tasted something slightly metallic on his tongue.

He concentrated on the envelope and the knife. The tip of the blade connected with something. Frank carefully opened the envelope wider and peered inside. There was something taped there. With the knife he tore the tape and turned the envelope upside down. A small spring-loaded device fell onto the kitchen table. It was no bigger than a matchbox and consisted of a mousetrap-like contraption with a thin needle attached. Frank had never seen anything like it before. After the prick to his finger he was wary, so he pushed it aside with the knife and opened the envelope even wider. There was something else inside. It was a single sheet of paper.

Frank's eyes were now starting to sting, and his vision was beginning to blur.

He emptied the piece of paper onto the table and opened it up with the knife. He wasn't going to risk being pricked again. The text on the letter was handwritten in block capitals. Frank's eyes were seeing double now, so he blinked it away and managed to read the words on the page.

'CONGRATULATIONS. YOU HAVE BEEN CHOSEN TO RECEIVE A SPECIAL PRIZE – A GIFT FROM A DENDROAPSIS POLYLEPIS. YOUR REWARD IS OBLIVION. SHOULD YOU DECIDE NOT TO ACCEPT THIS PRIZE, PHONE THE NUMBER BELOW AND REPEAT THESE FOUR SIMPLE WORDS – I WANT TO LIVE. '

Frank was baffled. He read the words again, but they still didn't make any sense.

Frank was now feeling drowsy, but he opened his eyes wide and concentrated on the number at the bottom of the page. It was a mobile number. He forced himself to stand up and retrieved his phone from the counter by the window. He stumbled back to the table and fell back down in the chair. He was now finding it difficult to breathe and he was sweating profusely. He managed to key in the number, but his hands were now numb and he was having trouble keeping hold of the phone. His vision was darkening and every time he inhaled it felt like somebody was sitting on his chest, squeezing the life out of him. He dropped the phone on the floor, and he didn't hear the voice on the other end of the line.

"Smith?"

Frank managed to reach the phone, picked it up and said in a feeble voice, "I want to live."

Then he dropped the phone again.

Frank Broadbent couldn't sit up any longer. He no longer had any feeling in his arms and legs. He collapsed to the floor and gasped for air but his mouth and nose wouldn't obey. His whole body was now covered in perspiration, but he felt extremely cold. With blurred vision he gazed up at the kitchen ceiling. His eyelids were heavy and he had difficulty keeping them open. The last thing he saw was a hazy damp patch on the ceiling above the sink, then his eyes closed, and he drifted off.

CHAPTER THREE

"Good morning, my Lovelies," the man with the lisp stroked his finger down the glass of the cage and gazed inside.

Two almost luminous-green coils were barely visible underneath a thick branch at the back of the cage. They were not moving. The man continued on to the next identical cage. This one contained his favourite – a brownish-grey creature much bigger than the green ones in the adjacent cage. It had pale-yellow stripes on its neck.

"The first winner ought to have received his prize by now," the man told his beloved Black Mamba. "And Jason Smith will have started to hear dead people. You did well. But the next winner has already been selected and I must get to work. I think we should ask Gaby if she would like to donate the next award, don't you?"

The man walked past the row of cages and stopped in front of one which was slightly bigger than the rest.

He tapped on the glass and smiled. "Hello, beautiful. It's time."

Inside the cage was what seemed at first glance to be just a head. A large yellow and brown triangular head with what looked like two tiny horns between its nostrils. On further inspection one could see that the head was attached to a thin neck. The rest of its body was concealed beneath pile of leaves.

"We've got work to do," the man took out a key and turned it in the keyhole on the side of the cage.

He grabbed what looked like a long sheep-hook from a bracket on the wall and stepped back from the cage. He put the end of the hook under the neck and lifted the serpent into the air.

"You become more beautiful every day," he looked directly into its dead eyes.

Gently he put his fingers around the slender neck and coaxed it out of the cage. He didn't wear safety gloves anymore. He and his 'Lovelies' had come to an understanding a long time ago. They were all well-fed, and in return they would oblige him in his peculiar requests.

He carried the Viper to the other end of the room. There was a workbench there, attached to which was a vice that held an odd looking clamp. A glass jar was held firmly onto the bench by the clamp. On top of the jar was a thin clear plastic film. The man deftly opened the snake's jaws and two extremely long fangs shot out. He punctured the plastic film with them, and the snake instinctively started to bite. Again and again it gnawed away at the edge of the jar. Soon, a milky liquid landed drop by drop into the jar.

"I think that's more than enough for now, Gaby," the man with the lisp said. He increased the pressure around the snake's neck and gently prised the fangs loose. He kissed the back of its head, placed it back in its cage and locked it again. The whole process had taken less than three minutes.

He went to inspect the morning's 'donation'. It was much more than he needed. He knew that the venom from the Gaboon Viper was not likely to kill his next *winner*, but that was not his intention on this occasion. The excruciating pain, severe shock and extensive tissue damage would be enough. And he was certain, Detective Sergeant Jason Smith would have already realised something was happening.

Something he was powerless to stop and something that was going to cause him unparalleled anguish and pain.

CHAPTER FOUR

Smith was still in high spirits after learning of Superintendent Smyth's karaoke prowess, when he knocked on DI Brownhill's office door. He opened the door and went inside as he'd always done. Bridge and Yang Chu were already seated. Smith made himself comfortable in the remaining chair facing the DI.

"A young girl was badly burned last light," Brownhill got straight down to business. "Fourteen years old. A faulty firework exploded in her face as soon as she'd lit it."

"Do we know where the firework came from?" Smith asked.

"We're looking into it."

"Probably the same place as the others," Bridge suggested.

This young girl was the latest in a string of people, mostly teenagers who'd been injured by illegal fireworks in the past month. Most of the fireworks had been identified as coming from a faulty batch imported from China, which had been due to be destroyed. The batch never made it to the incinerator – somebody helped themselves to the faulty fireworks, and now they were being sold on the street at a fraction of the price of the fireworks that complied with the Bureau of Standards' guidelines.

"I don't mean to moan," Yang Chu said. "But is investigating stolen fireworks actually in our job description?"

"People are getting hurt," Brownhill glared at him. "It is only a matter of time before somebody is killed. It is most definitely in your job description. The latest victim is going to be scarred for life. She suffered sixty-percent burns to her face. Her eyebrows and eyelashes were singed. Besides, I've had orders from higher up. This is a priority."

"And you can't argue with that," Smith said.

"What exactly happened?" Bridge asked.

"Most fireworks have a kind of delayed fuse-line – this fuse gives whoever lights it time to retreat before it explodes. This one's fuse didn't do that. It blew up immediately. We know where these fireworks came from, but we have no idea who has managed to get hold of them and, more importantly, who's selling them."

"How many fireworks are we talking about here?" Smith asked.

"A container arrived in Hull from China roughly two months ago. A small proportion of the fireworks in that container were inspected, didn't meet the bureau's approval and thus the whole lot was seized and due to be destroyed. Roughly thirty-thousand of all shapes and sizes."

"Bloody hell," Bridge said. "I wouldn't mind watching them blow that lot up. Fourth of July times ten."

"That's a lot of potentially deadly explosives on the streets," Smith thought out loud.

"It is," Brownhill agreed. "Most of the people who were injured were between the ages of ten and nineteen. They must be getting the fireworks from somewhere."

"Did forensics pick up anything from the container the fireworks were in?"

"Nothing. They were being kept at the container terminal until they could be transported and destroyed. The security at the terminal is adequate, but not state of the art. The lock on the container was broken – that much we do know, and the scene was covered with prints, but none of them gave us much."

"Prints from all over the world, no doubt," Smith said. "Has anything similar happened anywhere else in the country?"

"As far as I'm aware the injuries caused by these fireworks have been limited to York so far."

"Lucky us. What's the plan?"

"Get out there," Brownhill said. "Ask questions. Speaking to the latest victim is out of the question for the time being – she's in a lot of pain and she's going to have to endure a few months of skin grafts and the like, but I have a list of the others. Somebody must know who's selling these fireworks."

Smith and Yang Chu stood outside the address for the first name on their list. Steven Lund – a seventeen year old who was unfortunate enough to have purchased some of the faulty fireworks. According to the initial report, Steven wasn't the one who lit the mini rocket, but he was the one who happened to be standing where the rocket decided to go. Instead of flying skyward, the rocket had come loose from its bracket and ended up hurtling towards Steven Lund two feet above the ground, hitting his left leg and boring its way into his thigh.

"I've never seen the attraction of fireworks," Yang Chu said and rang the doorbell. "It's like sending burning money up into the air. What a waste."
"Not to mention the distress it causes the animals," Smith added. "I'm lucky – I've got two dogs who wouldn't even notice if a bomb went off next to them, but most dogs get really freaked out by fireworks. I don't know why they don't ban them altogether."
Yang Chu was about to say something when the door opened and a woman in her forties stood there. She was very tall and slim, with short black hair and the most unusual green eyes Smith had ever seen.
"Good morning," Smith spoke first. "Mrs Lund?"
"Yes," she replied. "Can I help you?"
Smith took out his ID. "DS Smith, and this is DC Yang Chu. We're here to speak to your son about the accident with the firework. Is Steven home?"
"You'd better come in."

She led Smith and Yang Chu into a small but cosy living room. The three-piece-suite was genuine leather and looked very expensive. A huge television set dominated one of the walls. On a sideboard in the corner stood a number of framed photographs. Something struck Smith as odd when he took a closer look. All of them depicted Mrs Lund and a young boy. They were the only two people in the photos.

She's divorced, he thought.

"Please take a seat," Mrs Lund said. "I'll call Steven for you. Would you like something to drink?"

"No thank you," Smith said.

A short while later a youngster limped into the room. He was tall like his mother, and he also had her unusual green eyes. He nodded to Smith and sat on the single-seater. His mother sat on the arm of his chair.

"How's the leg, Steven?" Smith asked.

The seventeen-year-old shrugged. "Still sore."

"Can you tell us what happened?"

"It was an accident," Steven said. "The rocket didn't go up – it whizzed along the ground and hit me in the leg."

"Where did you get the fireworks?" Smith didn't feel like beating around the bush.

"I didn't buy them."

"Could you please tell us who did?"

"What's this all about?" Steven's mother asked. "And why are the police involved?"

"Mrs Lund, I don't know if you are aware of this but what happened to Steven isn't a once-off incident. Over the past few weeks there have been numerous reports of accidents involving fireworks." Smith looked directly at Steven Lund. "Who bought the fireworks?"

"Dave," Steven said. "It was his eighteenth. We had a bit of a party."

"And do you know where he bought them?"

Steven shook his head. Smith could tell straight away he was lying.

"What do you do, Steven?" Yang Chu asked. "Are you working? College?"

"I'm in my second year at the sixth form," Steven replied.

"He's doing four A-Levels," his mother added, proudly. "All sciences."

"Impressive," Smith said. "Why aren't you at college now?"

"I've been given permission to study at home. I can't walk very well and besides, I'd much rather study on my own."

"I see," Smith said. "This friend of yours, Dave. We'll need his details."

"What for?" Steven's voice rose slightly in pitch.

"Because we believe somebody else is going to get hurt, and we need to find out where these fireworks are coming from."

"David Atkins," Steven's mother said, and her son glared at her. "I've never liked him. Bad influence."

"Mum," Steven's faced reddened.

"He is. I've told you to stay away from him. You need to concentrate on your studies if you want to get into a good University."

"Where can we find this David Atkins?" Smith asked her.

Mrs Lund looked at her son. "Steven, answer the detective's question."

Steven Lund remained quiet for a while. Defiant.

"Steven," his mother urged.

"He lives on Hull Road," Steven relented. "Number twenty-nine."

Smith stood up. "Thank you for your time. I hope your leg gets better soon."

CHAPTER FIVE

"Easy does it," the man with the lisp held the syringe in place.

He carefully pulled back the plunger and watched the milky liquid fill half the syringe. He removed the needle and attached another, much thinner one. He took the syringe with its special contents to his work bench. On the bench was a small mousetrap-like contraption with a thin needle attached. The idea had come to him during one of his many sleepless nights, and by the time dawn arrived the first one had been designed on paper. The concept was so simple, it was brilliant. It had taken a further two weeks to perfect it, but it had been worth it. The device in front of him consisted of a base, a spring attached to a metal ring and what the man with the lisp referred to as the rocket launcher – a thin, hollow tube of metal that thinned out even further to a tip with a sharp point. The hardest part of all was to design a plunger-device that would fit inside the needle, but a couple of days working with various nails and pins had solved that problem.

"Bitis Gabonica," the man mused, opened his mouth and, with his thumb and forefinger, felt the reason for his lisp.

Half of his tongue was missing. A few weeks earlier, he'd been milking Gaby, his Gaboon Viper and he'd lost his grip on her. Gaby had turned to face him and in a moment of madness he would never repeat he found himself sticking his tongue out at her. Gaby took this as an opportunity to strike and latched onto the tongue with her impressive fangs. The man knew too well the effect of the venom – he had anti-venom, but it wouldn't be enough to prevent some necrosis. He'd thrown his beloved Viper back in her cage, stuck his tongue out on the edge of a chopping board and sliced off as much as he could. The pain had been unbearable, but the nature of the snake's cytotoxic poison would mean he would have almost certainly lost it anyway. In a moment of inspiration, he'd spat out the blood that filled his mouth and used the knife to slice what remained of his tongue down the middle. Now, what remained was forked like that of his *lovelies*. He gazed at his reflection in the metal contraption and stuck out his tongue a few times in quick succession. A shiver of excitement rushed through his whole body.

The man with the lisp steadied his hands and injected the milky-white venom into the metal tube until it spilled out. He positioned it over his *plunger* and pulled the spring back. He opened the padded A4 envelope – the note was already inside, and taped his contraption carefully underneath where he had already written, 'OPEN HERE'. He was careful to make sure the spring was fully loaded before he attached the thin wire to it, taped the wire to the inside of where the envelope sealed, and pressed it down tightly. As an extra precaution, he taped up the seal – he didn't want the envelope opening before it had served its purpose.

The man with the lisp opened up the York telephone directory, closed his eyes, and turned the pages. With his eyes still closed, he placed his finger on the page. He opened his eyes and smiled. He liked the sound of the name he'd chosen.

M. Russell. It was fate.

The winner of the next *prize* was going to receive a gift from the Russell's Viper, the snake responsible for more deaths than any other.

The man with the lisp wrote the address on the front of the envelope, moistened four first-class stamps with a wet sponge, and stuck them on the envelope. He'd seen a documentary once about a real-life murder where the killer was eventually found because forensics officers had pulled DNA from saliva on a stamp. He repeated the process with two more stamps. He wanted to make absolutely sure the envelope and its contents reached the next *winner*. He picked up the envelope, grabbed his car keys and left the house. It was only when he'd placed the envelope on the back seat of his car that he removed the rubber gloves. He realised he was being overly cautious

– the envelope would pass through many hands on its way to its destination, but he wanted to make absolutely sure nothing about it could lead back to him.

Not just yet.

There would be plenty of time for that later.

The drive to Whitby would take forty five minutes depending on traffic. The man with the lisp turned the key in the ignition and drove away from his house. He knew he'd left it too late to ensure the next *winner* would receive their *prize* tomorrow, but he had no regrets.

All good things come to those who wait.

And he had waited long enough.

CHAPTER SIX

David Atkins wasn't at home when Smith and Yang Chu had paid him a visit, but they'd been advised as to his probable whereabouts by his mother – a woman who seemed to think it was perfectly acceptable for an eighteen-year-old to frequent a pub on a Monday morning.

"She wasn't exactly in the running for mother of the year," Yang Chu commented as they made their way towards the city centre. "No wonder there's so much crime in this place. Who the hell lets their kid go to the pub on a Monday morning?"

"He's eighteen," Smith pointed out. "Kids stop being kids at around age thirteen these days."

"Thank you for that, old wise one. It's still not quite right though, is it?"

"No, it's not." Smith agreed.

"Do you think this Atkins bloke knows anything about the illegal fireworks?"

"Let's go and find out."

Smith parked in the car park of the Green Acres pub and stopped the engine.

"Which one of us do you think looks less like police?" he asked.

"What sort of question is that?"

"If we go in there and start asking this David Atkins bloke about where he bought his fireworks, what do you think is going to happen?"

"I don't know," Yang Chu said. "He'll exercise his right to the fifth?"

"They show far too much American crap on TV these days. You mean he'll keep quiet?"

"That's what I just said. And to answer your first question, no offence, but you've got detective written all over you. You're the one who's been in all the papers, remember?"

"I haven't been in all the papers."

"You asked me a question and I answered it."

Smith thought for a moment. "No, you're right. You go in there alone."

"And do what?"

"Ask David Atkins where you can buy some cheap fireworks."

"And you think he's going to tell me?"

"Use your imagination – tell him you're organising a kid's party. Tell him you need some fireworks to celebrate Vietnamese New Year."

"Did I just hear right? I'm second generation Vietnamese. My mother's from Yorkshire. I was born here, which is more than I can say for you."

"Alright," Smith said. "Calm down."

"Besides, Vietnamese New Year is 25 January."

"And do you think someone like David Atkins is aware of that? Like I said, use your imagination."

Yang Chu got out of the car, slammed the door behind him and went inside the pub. The interior of the Green Acres was exactly what he expected it to be like – dark and dingy with a strong stench of stale beer in the air. David Atkins' mother had shown them a photograph of her son and Yang Chu spotted him immediately. He knew if he walked straight over to Atkins, it would arouse suspicion, so he made his way to the bar.

"Yeh?" the barman said.

Yang Chu translated this to mean, 'what would you like to drink?'

"Coke, please."

"One, fifty," the barman put the drink on the bar.

Yang Chu paid him, took a sip of the coke and glanced over at David Atkins. He was a skinny youth with very bad acne. His hair had been cut in an army-style crew cut, and he had a bruise the size of two-pound coin on one cheek. He was with two other youths of around the same age as him.

Use your imagination.

Smith's words were still fresh in his head, but Yang Chu didn't have a clue how he was going to play it. He took a long drink from his glass, and walked over to David Atkins' table.

Atkins' whole demeanour changed when Yang Chu approached. The DC had seen it plenty of times before. David Atkins had automatically assumed a defensive stance.

"Morning, lads," Yang Chu said. "I'm looking for Dave."

"There's no Dave here," it was Atkins who spoke.

"Dave Atkins?" Yang Chu said, all the time holding eye contact with Atkins.

"Who wants to know?" one of Atkins' friends asked.

He was a short man with hair so greasy it looked like it had never been washed.

"I need a favour," Yang Chu said. "And I was told that David Atkins could help me. I'm willing to pay. How about I get a round in, and if you can help me, great. But if you can't then I'll just bugger off and find someone who can. No harm done."

A couple of minutes later, Yang Chu sat next to the man with the chip-pan hair. There were three pints of lager and a coke on the table.

"What do you want?" David Atkins asked and picked up his pint.

"Fireworks," Yang Chu came right out with it.

"And what makes you think I can help you with fireworks?" Atkins was still on the defensive.

"That's just what I've heard."

"Just what you've heard? Are you police?"

Yang Chu started to laugh. "I've been called some things in my life, but that's got to be the worst. Can you help me or not?"

A smile appeared on Atkins' face. "What do you need?"

Yang Chu decided to go with Smith's story about Vietnamese New Year. He told David Atkins he would need enough fireworks for at least a two hour display.

"That's a lot of fireworks," Atkins pointed out when Yang Chu was finished.

"I know," Yang Chu said. "And it would cost a fortune if I bought them from the shops."

"Vietnamese New Year you say?"

Yang Chu nodded.

David Atkins took out a mobile phone and pressed a few keys. For a few agonising moments, Yang Chu wondered if he was using Google to look up Vietnamese New Year. Atkins stopped typing, placed his phone on the table and finished what was left in his glass. The phone beeped, and he picked it up. He studied the screen, put the phone down again and looked at Yang Chu.

"I might just be able to help you. But I'll need a deposit."

"A deposit?" Yang Chu remembered he only had twenty pounds in his wallet.

"Good will and all that."

"How much?"

"Two hundred," Atkins said. "Then another two hundred when you get the fireworks. A decent two hour display would normally cost well over a grand. And these are good quality fireworks."

"I'll have to go and draw some cash," Yang Chu told him. "I haven't got enough on me."

"There's a cash machine just round the corner," Atkins informed him. "I'll be here for another couple of hours."

CHAPTER SEVEN

Smith watched from his car as Yang Chu left the pub and headed off down the street without even glancing in his direction. He knew straight away that Yang Chu was on to something. He started the engine and followed a short distance behind. When he was sure he was no longer visible from the Green Acres pub he caught up with Yang Chu and stopped.

"He wants money," Yang Chu said when he'd got in the car. "I didn't have enough on me. And I didn't know if he'd be watching to see if I was with someone."

He told Smith everything that had happened inside the pub.

"Nice work," Smith said. "We're getting closer, and I told you he wouldn't have a clue about Vietnamese New Year. How much does he need?"

"Two hundred quid for a deposit and another two hundred when I get the fireworks."

"Did he mention who's supplying?"

"Unfortunately not."

"It doesn't matter," Smith said. "As soon as everything is set up, we can follow him. How long have we got?"

"He'll be in the pub for a couple of hours."

"Then we've got plenty of time to authorise the money and the operation."

Smith's mobile phone started to ring. He took it out and handed it to Yang Chu. "Can you answer it?"

"It's DS Bridge," Yang Chu said and pressed 'answer'.

"Smith," Bridge said. "We've spoken to all the people on the list and we haven't found a thing."

"It's Yang Chu," the DC told Bridge. "Smith's driving. We may have a decent lead."

"Good, because everybody we spoke to seemed scared stiff of this firework merchant and wouldn't tell us anything. What have you got?"

"We spoke to one of the teenagers who got injured, and this kid's mother told us about a David Atkins. Wannabe hard man, nothing more. I've just finished speaking with him and we've arranged a time to make a deal. I think he could lead us straight to the main player in all this."

"How the hell did you do that?" Bridge asked.

"By using my imagination. We're on our way back in – I need cash, and we need to go through how we're going to play it."

Twenty minutes later the team gathered in the small conference room. As Whitton had a few days off, PC Baldwin had been called in to assist. She'd helped out on plenty of operations in the past. Smith had filled Brownhill in on what they had so far, and now the DI was sitting at the head of the table with a file in front of her and a rare smile on her face.

"It's been one of those days," Brownhill began. "One of those we so seldom get, yet when we do, we need to take full advantage of. Smith and Yang Chu have a positive lead in the investigation into the stolen consignment of defective fireworks. Smith."

"We got a bit of luck," Smith admitted. "And DC Yang Chu pushed that luck and struck gold." He glanced at his watch. "In an hour's time I want all of you in position outside the Green Acres pub on Jenkins Street. Yang Chu will go inside the pub, hand his guy the deposit for the fireworks, and that will be the last part he plays."

"Who's his 'guy'? PC Baldwin asked.

"David Atkins," Smith told her. "Nothing special. No form. Seems to think of himself as a player heading upwards, that's all. He's the link between Yang Chu and the main man. Once the money has been exchanged, we hope Mr Atkins will lead us straight to our firework merchant."

"And if he doesn't?" Bridge said.

"We'll cross that bridge when we come to it, but I get the feeling our Mr Atkins will want to collect his cut as quickly as possible."

"Any questions?"

"Just one," Yang Chu said.

"Go ahead," it was DI Brownhill.

"I had to buy two cokes and three pints of lager at the Green Acres, Ma'am" Yang Chu told her. "It cost me fifteen quid. Can I claim that back?"

Brownhill laughed. "I don't see that being a problem. The cash for the deposit and balance on the fireworks has been authorised, so if there isn't anything further, let's get moving."

Yang Chu parked his Ford Focus in the car park of the Green Acres. Smith had driven with him. Bridge and Baldwin were in position at the back of the pub where Smith had learned there was a service entrance. A team of four uniformed police officers in two cars had been placed on standby, should things get out of hand.

"Are you ready?" Smith asked Yang Chu.

Yang Chu patted the wad of notes in his pocket and nodded. "Ready as I'll ever be."

"This could be a real feather in your cap if everything goes to plan."

"Let's hope it goes to plan, then."

Yang Chu opened the door, got out of the car and headed for the entrance of the pub.

Smith watched as he went inside. He picked up his mobile phone and brought up Bridge's number.

"In position," Bridge answered the call. "We do have radios you know."

"I hate the things. Yang Chu has just gone inside. Stand by."

Smith waited, all the time watching the open door of the pub. After a few minutes he started to think something had gone wrong. Yang Chu was taking far too long.

Something was wrong.

* * *

Yang Chu sat at David Atkins' table for the second time that day. Atkins was definitely more intoxicated than he had been earlier, and one of Atkins' friends had left. He was sitting with the greasy-haired youth.

"I've got your money," Yang Chu told him and placed an envelope on the table.

Atkins observed it with bleary eyes, picked it up and stuffed it into the side pocket of his jacket. He stood up and blinked a few times. He started to walk away.

"Where are you going?" Yang Chu asked him.

"Gents. You don't think I'm going to count the money in front of the whole pub do you?"

Yang Chu looked around him. It was Monday lunchtime and the pub was empty, apart from an elderly man reading a newspaper at a table across from the bar.

"There's nobody else here," he said.

"That's the way it is," Atkins told him and made his way towards the Gents.

Yang Chu began to panic. He knew they had people in position front and back. What if there was another way out of the pub – via the window in the toilets. If Atkins' greasy-haired friend wasn't sitting with him, he could alert Smith, but he couldn't risk taking out his phone now. His fears were allayed a couple of minutes later when David Atkins returned and sat back down.

"It's all there," he said. "You can go now."

"What about the fireworks?" Yang Chu said. "How do I know you won't just run off with my money?"

"You don't. But that wouldn't be too good for me and my future endeavours would it?"

He started to laugh. "Future endeavors. I like that. Come back here at four this afternoon with the rest of the money. I'll meet you in the car park. And don't try anything stupid. I'll know if something's not right – I have a nose for that kind of thing."

CHAPTER EIGHT

Four o' clock was still a couple of hours away. Smith decided he would wait alone to see where David Atkins went. He couldn't risk Yang Chu being seen around the pub. Bridge and Baldwin were to remain at the back of the Green Acres in case Atkins decided to exit there.

"What am I supposed to do in the meantime?" Yang Chu asked.

"I told you earlier in the briefing," Smith said. "You've done your bit. The deal isn't going to take place is it? All we need to do is follow Atkins and find out where he goes to fetch the fireworks. Get a lift back to the station with uniform. And keep your mobile close – I'll keep you informed and call you if we need you."

Yang Chu didn't look happy. "Just look after my car. I know what your driving can be like at times."

"I'll treat it like my own."

"That's what worries me. And no smoking. This is a non-smoking car."

"Received loud and clear. Get out of here."

Smith kept his eyes trained on the entrance to the Green Acres pub. A surprising amount of people arrived and went inside. It was early Monday afternoon and the pub appeared to be slowly filling up. For some reason it made Smith feel slightly depressed. It just didn't seem right somehow. They were people of all ages. Why weren't they at work?

The door of the pub opened, and Smith spotted somebody he recognised from the photograph he'd been shown earlier in the day. It was David Atkins and he was alone. He staggered out and almost lost his balance on the step outside the pub. He looked around in a way Smith had seen numerous times before – the way somebody looks around when they're up to something. He headed away from the car park in the opposite direction from the city centre. Smith realised it would be difficult to follow him in Yang Chu's car, so he got out, locked the door and set off about fifty feet behind.

It was starting to get dark as Smith passed the old Post Office building and they headed towards what Smith knew to be low-cost housing estates. He rubbed his hands together, took out his phone and called Bridge. "He's heading for the Richmond Estate. Yang Chu has gone back with uniform. I'm on foot, so can you organise back-up in the area right away?"

"Yang Chu is with us. And you shouldn't be by yourself in that part of town," Bridge said. "It's starting to get dark."

"Didn't you just hear what I said about back-up? I'll let you know as soon as I've got an address, but it looks like it's definitely on the Richmond."

He rang off. David Atkins was still fifty feet ahead. Smith knew Bridge was right – the Richmond Estate wasn't exactly a safe place to be after dark. The houses he passed all looked the same – unkempt, with rubbish piled up in the gardens and rusty old cars dumped outside.

David Atkins slowed down so Smith hid in a driveway and ducked behind an old Ford Capri that would probably never see the road again. Atkins turned around and looked right and left. Smith watched him stagger up the drive and head around the side of the house. Smith took out his phone and dialled Bridge's number again.

"Where are you?"

"Already on the Richmond," Bridge told him. "Where are you?"

"King Street. I'm outside number 41 and Atkins has gone round the back a few houses up."

"We're just round the corner. How do you want to play it?"

"I'm not sure why he went to the back of the house, but I want someone there just in case."

"The back of King Street is just alleyways," Bridge told him. "I'll get uniform in position there, and we'll meet you at the front."

"I'm hiding behind a dead Ford Capri. Hurry up."

30 seconds later, Smith heard the sound of a car approaching slowly. He spotted the headlights then they were turned off.

Bridge, he thought.

This was DS Bridge's idea of stealth mode – he cut the headlights fifty metres from his destination. The car slowed down further and came to a halt opposite where Smith was crouching. Bridge and Baldwin got out from the front and Yang Chu appeared from the back. Smith emerged from his hiding place and walked up to the car.

"What are you doing here?" he asked Yang Chu. "I thought I told you to go back to the station."

"Couldn't get hold of uniform," Yang Chu said. "I waited at the back of the pub with Bridge and Baldwin. What's the plan?"

"Atkins went round the back. I'm not sure why he did that, but I reckon we do the same."

"Maybe he didn't want to be seen from the street," Baldwin suggested.

"No," Bridge had a brightness in his eyes he often got when he'd thought of something. "A shed. I think they've got a shed out the back."

"What makes you say that?" Yang Chu asked.

"Think about it. If you'd nicked a container-load of dodgy fireworks, where would you keep them? In the house, knowing full well they could possibly blow up at any time, or outside in a lock-up or a shed?"

"Bridge has a point," Smith said. "Is uniform in place at the back?"

"Two cars," Baldwin said. "One at either end of the alleyway that runs the whole length of the road."

"Good. Let's go then."

Smith went first with Yang Chu. The driveway David Atkins had walked up belonged to number 47. There were no cars parked there. The lights were off inside the house.

"Do you have a torch?" Smith whispered to Yang Chu.

"Of course," Yang Chu took out a small penlight.

There was a narrow path that led past the left hand side of the house.

"That's where he must have gone," Smith said and turned to Bridge and Baldwin. "You two stay here in case he gets past us and tries to make a run for it. He might go inside the house and try to get out the front door."

Smith and Bridge moved cautiously past the side of the house into what could only be described as a back yard. It was winter yet Smith knew no grass would ever grow here. Something crunched under his foot. Broken glass. Yang Chu shone his torch on something at the back of the yard. Bridge had been right – a small wooden shed measuring roughly three by three metres stood facing the house. There were no windows, the door was closed but a faint light could be seen through a crack in the door frame. "There's someone in there," Yang Chu said. "I'll go in first. No offence, Sarge, but my self-defence skills are a bit more up to date than yours." Smith had no arguments there. He nodded to Yang Chu, the young DC approached the door of the shed and took hold of the handle. The padlock that usually secured the door was hanging from a hook next to the handle. The door wasn't locked. Yang Chu switched off his torch and put it back in his pocket. He wanted to make sure he had two free hands at his disposal. He nodded back to Smith and yanked the door open.

CHAPTER NINE

David Atkins and another older-looking man were sitting on some boxes inside the shed. They each had a bottle of beer in their hand. Atkins' friend shot up when Yang Chu burst in.

"Who the fuck are you?"

Atkins appeared to be a bit slower on the uptake. He'd obviously carried on drinking since his session at the Green Acres and it took him a while to recognise Yang Chu as the man who wanted to celebrate Vietnamese New Year with faulty fireworks.

The boxes the two men were sitting on were brightly coloured and covered with pictures of badly drawn fireworks. They'd definitely come to the right place.

"Police," Smith said. "Please put the bottles down and stand with your hands behind your backs."

"Piss off," Atkins' friend said.

Smith had expected as much. There was something familiar about the man – he looked like somebody Smith had met before.

He looked at the bottle in his hand raised it in the air and tried to smash it against the wooden wall of the shed. There was a dull thud, but the bottle remained intact.

"Physics," Smith said. "The wood isn't dense enough. You'd have better results if you smacked yourself on the head with it."

The man appeared to be considering Smith's suggestion when Yang Chu moved in. The man swung the bottle in the DC's direction, Yang Chu stepped to the side and gripped the hand holding it. He used the momentum of the swing and yanked the arm towards him. There was a sickening crunch, the man screamed, and the bottle fell to the floor.

"That's going to be a bit sore for a while," Smith said. "Now, can we start again? Please stand with your hands behind your back."

This time there were no arguments. They were both secured with handcuffs in seconds.

"What's all this?" Smith pointed to the boxes on the floor.

"Looks like you're a bit late for Guy Fawkes' Night," Yang Chu added.

"They're not mine," David Atkins' friend claimed. "They were here when we moved in."

The petty criminal's capacity for lying never ceased to amaze Smith. Even in the face of overwhelming evidence they would persist.

"I don't even know what's in the boxes," the man added.

Smith sighed, and took out his cigarettes and lighter. He pretended to light a cigarette and looked at David Atkins. "Smoke?" He threw the unlit cigarette in Atkins' direction. It landed between two of the boxes on the floor.

"Are you trying to blow us all up?" the other man screamed and looked to where he thought the cigarette had landed.

His eyes were bulging.

"Get out, both of you," Smith said. "And don't be a pair of idiots. You don't think there are just the two of us do you?"

He lit a cigarette for real outside number 47 King Road and watched as David Atkins and his friend were helped into a police car and driven away.

"What are we going to do with the fireworks?" Bridge asked.

"Forensics will want to go over them," Smith replied. "To make sure they are the ones that were stolen from the container in Hull, and then they'll be destroyed."

"Did you see that bloke's face when he thought you were about to blow us all into the next world?" Yang Chu said. "I must admit I thought you'd lost the plot a bit back there myself."

"Do we know who the other man is?" Smith asked.

"The next-door-neighbour came out while we were waiting," Bridge said. "Nosy bastard. He asked us what we were doing there. Apparently it's a man by the name of Darren Maude who lives there. We're still not sure if it's him we arrested."

"Darren Maude?" Smith thought out loud. "The face and the name really do ring a bell. I'm sure we've met somewhere before."

"Let's go and find out shall we?" Bridge said. "I suppose we'll have to wait for legal. In my experience, scrotes like them always think they're entitled to legal representation."

"They are," Smith reminded him. "We live in a mad world."

Smith and Yang Chu drove back to the station in silence. Yang Chu glanced across at his colleague every now and again. Smith had a look on his face Yang Chu couldn't translate – he was staring intently at the windscreen in front of him, and he didn't blink.

"Are you alright, Sarge?" Yang Chu broke the silence.

"What?" Smith jerked his head towards him.

"You haven't said a word since we got in the car."

"I didn't realise talking was obligatory. I've seen that Maude bloke before. There's something far too familiar about him. I just can't put my finger on what it is and it's pissing me off."

"It'll come to you."

Smith went inside the station and headed straight for the canteen. He chose the strongest coffee he could find in the machine and took it to the table by the window.

Darren Maude, he thought. *Where have I heard that name before?*
Nothing came to him. He gazed out at the lights of the city. The Minster was lit up as usual. York Minster. Smith's favourite building in the whole world. He'd lost count of how many times he'd walked past it. He remembered

when he first came to York and his Gran had taken him inside for the first time. It had been like nothing he had ever seen before.

York Minster.

A snippet of a memory was trying to force its way to the top of the other thoughts in his head.

York Minster and Smith's Gran.

Smith left the coffee untouched and ran out of the canteen.

CHAPTER TEN

"Where are the two men who were just brought in?" Smith asked the custody officer on duty. "David Atkins and Darren Maude?"

The custody officer frowned at him. "Atkins is in 3 and Maude's in 6. Legal won't be able to make it until the morning, so they're going to be our guests for the night."

"I need to speak to Darren Maude."

"Didn't you hear what I just said? Legal Aid won't be here until tomorrow morning."

"I don't give a hoot about legal aid. I need to speak to him now."

"Out of the question. You know the rules."

Smith did know the rules. He'd broken most of them in his career, and he wasn't about to stop now. "I just need two minutes. I need to ask him something important."

"I know all about you, DS Smith – you think you can do what you please, but like I told you, it's out of the question."

"What's out of the question?" a voice came from nowhere.

It was Chalmers.

"What's out of the question?" the DCI asked again.

"DS Smith asked if he could talk to one of the suspects brought in on the firework thing, sir. I can't let him interview the suspect alone."

"It's not an interview," Smith was getting really annoyed. He looked at Chalmers. "Boss, you can be present while I talk to him."

"I don't see why not," Chalmers agreed. "But I need a favour in return."

"Deal." Smith started to walk towards the holding cells before the anally-retentive duty officer had a chance to argue.

"What's going on?" Chalmers caught up with him. "Why the urgency?"

"Do you remember something I did a while ago? About ten years ago. It landed me with a suspension."

"That doesn't exactly narrow it down."

"A pair of thugs broke into my house – we caught the bastards but then it turned out one of them was the one responsible for the death of my Gran."

Smith had been celebrating coming top of his class three years into a law degree. Not far from the Minster, his Gran was mugged. A youth grabbed her handbag and shoved her to the floor, resulting in her breaking her hip. She never recovered and died three weeks later. His name was Steven Maude. The incident was what had made Smith give up on the law degree and join the police instead. He'd watched as some smarmy defence lawyer had talked his way towards Steven Maude receiving a paltry sentence for being instrumental in the death of the person Smith loved more than anything else on earth. Maude walked away from prison after just over a year.

"I seem to remember you giving the scrote a damn good kicking," Chalmers remembered it well. "You were lucky to get away with a suspension. What's this got to do with this fireworks business?"

"I was sure one of the men we brought in looked familiar. He said his name's Darren Maude, but I think he's lying. He's the spitting image of the bloke who mugged my Gran."

"And what are you planning on doing in there? Finishing off the job?"

"Of course not. I've grown up a bit since then. I just want to ask him a few questions. Nothing untoward, boss."

"There'd better not be."

The custody officer reluctantly unlocked the door to holding cell 6 and Smith and Chalmers went inside. Darren Maude was sitting on the bed. He was holding his right arm with his left. Smith stared at him – he was certain this was the same man who had mugged his Gran.

"How's the arm, Darren?" he asked. "If that's even your real name."

Maude looked up. "What are you going on about? I could have you up for assault for this."

He held up his injured arm.

"Assaulting a police officer is a more serious charge, Darren. Or should I call you Steven?"

Maude's pasty face turned even paler. "What did you say?"

"Steven Maude. I believe we've met."

Maude made a move to stand up, Chalmers took a step closer to him, and he seemed to change his mind.

"Don't you even mention his name," Maude said. "You're not fit to mention that name."

"Steven Maude," Smith carried on undeterred. "Scumbag and murderer."

Chalmers' presence didn't work this time. Maude got off the bed and flung himself at Smith. Smith wasn't expecting it and he was forced back into the wall. Chalmers moved in, managed to drag him off and shoved him back on the bed.

"I think that's enough, don't you?" he said to Smith.

"My brother was not a murderer," Maude whimpered from the bed.

Smith turned and looked him in the eyes. "Your brother?"

"He was two years older than me. He was not a murderer."

Something about Darren Maude's whole demeanour had changed. He was no longer a defiant criminal – he was almost childlike in his protestations.

Smith realised something else – Maude had referred to his brother in the past tense. "What happened to him?"

"He got knifed outside a pub one night," Maude said. "He was dead before he even reached the hospital. It wasn't his fault."

"It never is, is it? I'm not sorry about your brother, Darren. And the life expectancy for people like him is considerably shorter than average, but I am sorry that it looks like you're heading down the same path. As far as I'm aware, this is the first time you've been in trouble with the law. Get out before it's too late."

Smith walked out of the room leaving an open-mouthed Chalmers in his wake.

CHAPTER ELEVEN

Bob Chalmers found Smith outside in the car park smoking a cigarette. The DCI lit his own and shivered in the late afternoon cold.

"Are you alright?"

"I am, yes, boss. I think I'm getting old."

"Maturing is the word. Like a fine wine."

Smith started to laugh. "More like a mouldy cheese in my case. What was that favour you wanted?"

"Favour?"

"You said you need a favour in return. What is it?"

"Shit," Chalmers said and started to cough. "I'm the old one here. My memory is getting worse. We had a missing person call come in. The missing man was only reported missing a few hours ago, but the person who rang in is an old friend of mine. Tommy Bonner. He owns a franchise for one of the chain restaurants in town. Anyway, his manager didn't show up for work today. He isn't answering his phone, and Tommy's worried about him."

"He's only been gone a few hours," Smith reminded him. "That's hardly a missing person."

"That's what I said. But Tommy is convinced. This manager has been with them for two years – he's never had a day off sick and he's never been late. Tommy reckons it's not like him to not let them know where he is, and he's concerned he might have hurt himself or worse."

"Who is this missing person?"

"Bloke by the name of Frank Broadbent. Thirty six years old, so it's unlikely he's had a heart attack or fallen and can't get up."

"What exactly do you want me to do about it? You know it'll be a total waste of time, don't you?"

"A favour's a favour. He lives on Bartlett Street. Number 34. That's on your way home isn't it? Just check it out. Knock on the door. Have a quick look around. You're probably right, but I promised Tommy we'd look into it."

Smith turned into Bartlett Street and stopped outside number 34. He knew this was going to be a complete waste of time, and had it been anyone else but Chalmers who'd asked him he would have refused. He'd lost count of how many times The DCI had stuck his neck out for him, and if his memory served him right, this was the first time he had actually reciprocated. He got out of the car and pulled his jacket further up his neck. The temperature had surely dipped below freezing now. The lights were out in number 34 and the curtains were open which straight away suggested there was nobody at home. A streetlight directly opposite shed ample light on the path that led to the house. Smith walked up and rang the doorbell. He waited a while and rang it again, this time keeping his finger on it longer than necessary. If there was somebody at home, he knew this would definitely attract their attention.
Nothing.

Smith tried the door. It was locked. He thought about what Chalmers had told him about the suspected missing person. Thirty six year old male. Roughly the same age as he was.
Old enough to look after himself, and definitely not somebody to presume is a missing person after only a few hours. Smith was wasting his time. He'd done as he was asked, and now he was going to turn around and go home.

Smith heard a sound directly across the road. It sounded like a car door being slammed. He heard the engine starting and the headlights were turned on, illuminating Frank Broadbent's garden even more. The lights shone right through the aluminium door with its two panes of glass – they lit up something at the end of the hallway, and it was something that caught Smith's eye immediately.

Something that definitely wasn't supposed to be there.

The car across the road pulled out of the driveway, turned left and carried on down the road, leaving the house in darkness again. Smith took out his mobile phone and switched on the torch app. It was a new app and the torch was incredibly bright. He shone it in the direction of where he thought he's seen something, and there it was, lying on the floor about ten metres away. Smith had seen enough dead bodies during his time in the police force to know what he was looking at right now.

He tried to think quickly. The right thing to do would be to get hold of forensics and wait in the car until they arrived. The right thing to do would be to round up the team and wait for them to arrive too. Entering a potential crime scene alone was not the right thing to do, but what if it wasn't a potential crime scene? What if it was just thirty-six-year old man who had collapsed and needed urgent medical attention?

Smith had enough justification to satisfy his conscience. He opened up his car boot and returned to the front door of the house armed with a hefty car jack. He turned his face away from the glass and smashed the bottom pane. He removed the remaining glass from the frame and crept through the gap. He took out the pair of SOC gloves he always carried with him, put them on and fumbled on the wall to find a light switch. He found what he was looking for by the open kitchen door, the light flickered and illuminated what was on the floor of the kitchen. The first thing that occurred to Smith was the man lying there was beyond medical attention, and the second was it was definitely time to call it in.

Grant Webber appeared fifteen minutes later. The head of forensics always seemed to be the first to arrive on the scene.

"What have we got?" he asked Smith outside the house.

"Dead man," Smith replied. "I assume it's Frank Broadbent."

"And what exactly are you doing here?"

Smith told him about the missing person report and how Chalmers had asked him for a favour.

"Do you think he was murdered?" Webber asked when Smith had finished.

"I don't think so. I'd say the poor bastard had a heart attack."

Webber eyed the smashed pane of glass in the door. "Your handiwork I suppose?"

"I saw him lying on the kitchen floor," Smith told him. "I didn't know if he was dead or if he'd just collapsed, so I went in to try and help him. I haven't touched anything inside."

"Good," Webber growled and went inside the house.

Brownhill, Bridge and Yang Chu arrived in the DI's car. They got out and walked up to Smith.

"The DCI told me about the missing person report," Brownhill said. "Do we know what happened yet?"

"Your better half is in there now," Smith said. "We'll know more when we get a path report, but if I were to hazard a guess, I'd say he had a heart attack. I found him lying on the kitchen floor."

"There's an ambulance on the way. Let's have a look shall we?"

Smith followed her inside. Grant Webber was looking at the dead man on the floor. Smith walked up for a closer look. The man he assumed to be Frank Broadbent was lying on his back. His eyes had rolled back in their sockets and now only the whites were visible. His face had a disturbing bluish hue to it and his mouth was wide open. Both hands were around his neck. A mobile phone was on the floor next to him.

"What do you think?" Smith asked Webber.

"I'm no expert," the head of forensics replied. "But the way his hands are around his neck and the open mouth would suggest he was fighting for breath at the end."

"Which means?" Brownhill asked.

"I don't think it was a heart attack. I've seen someone have a heart attack and their hands were pressed to the chest not around the neck. And I think he panicked and tried to call for help. But it looks like he didn't quite make it in time. There are no obvious signs he was attacked by anyone. No blood I can see. The path guys will be able to tell us more, but I'd say this was natural causes."

Smith looked around the kitchen. It was incredibly neat and tidy. There were no unwashed dishes in the sink, the surfaces were all spotless and all of the crockery and utensils were in pristine condition. He spotted a pile of letters on the table in the middle of the room. Most of them were unopened, but there were a couple of what looked like final demands put to one side. A padded A4 envelope with Frank Broadbent's name and address written in block capitals on the front lay next to them. There was a strange-looking metal object on top of the envelope.

"Webber," Smith shouted. "Come and have a look at this."

"What is it?" Webber said.

"What the hell is that?" Smith pointed to the mystery contraption.

Webber picked up the metal object. It was barely an inch in length with a spring attached to a ring on top of a metal base. A thin needle-like spike was fastened to the wire on the spring.

"I've never seen anything like it before," Webber said and placed it in a clear evidence bag. "It's probably not relevant to how the bloke died, but I'll have a look at it anyway."

Smith spotted something on the floor next to the fridge. It was a sheet of paper. He picked it up and read what was written on it. It didn't make any sense at all. He read it again and was about to dismiss it as nonsense when two things occurred to him. He recalled the phone call he'd received that morning. A prank call, he'd put it down to, but when he read the mobile phone number at the bottom of the sheet of paper his stomach warmed, and his heart started to beat faster. There was a dead man a few feet away from him – a man he'd never met before, yet his phone number was on a sheet of paper on the floor of the man's kitchen.

CHAPTER TWELVE

"Check the call history on his phone," Smith said to Webber and realised he was shaking.

"All in good time," Webber told him.

"Do it now. This phone is new to me. I don't know how to bring up the last number."

"I'll do it," Bridge offered.

He took the phone, pressed the button on the front and frowned.

"Fingerprint locked. It needs a fingerprint."

"We've got his fingerprint right there," Smith pointed to the dead man on the floor.

"I can't do that," Bridge said. "That's just sick."

Smith grabbed the phone from Bridge, bent down and picked up Frank Broadbent's cold hand and pressed his index finger against the screen. The phone came to life and Smith handed it back to Bridge.

"Now find out who he phoned last."

It seemed to take forever. Smith watched as Bridge tapped on the screen of the phone, and then his eyes widened.

"I recognise this number," he said.

"It's my mobile number," Smith told him.

"What exactly is going on here?" Brownhill asked.

"I've never met this man before in my life," Smith said. "Yet I think he phoned me this morning."

"What did he want?" the DI asked.

"I thought it was a prank call. I answered and I thought I heard him say *I want to live*. His voice was very quiet."

"I want to live?" Brownhill said.

Smith picked up the sheet of paper and handed it to her. Brownhill read it and put it back on the table.

"Why is your mobile phone number on here?" she asked. "And what is all this about claiming a prize?"

"Let me see," Webber picked it up.

'CONGRATULATIONS. YOU HAVE BEEN CHOSEN TO RECEIVE A SPECIAL PRIZE – A GIFT FROM A DENDROAPSIS POLYLEPIS. YOUR REWARD IS OBLIVION. SHOULD YOU DECIDE NOT TO ACCEPT THIS PRIZE, PHONE THE NUMBER BELOW AND REPEAT THESE FOUR SIMPLE WORDS – I WANT TO LIVE. '

"I want to live?" he looked at Smith. "You said that's what he said to you?"

"I think so. What the hell is going on here?"

"And what on earth is a Dendroapsis whatever?" Bridge asked.

"I'll Google it," Yang Chu offered.

He took out his phone, opened up his web browser and typed 'Dendroapsis Polyepsis' into the search bar. He scrolled down and frowned.

"Black Mamba," he said.

"Black Mamba?" Smith repeated.

"It's a snake."

"I know what a Black Mamba is, Yang Chu. What I don't know is why the Latin name of a deadly snake is written on a piece of paper with my phone number on the bottom, and why is that sheet of paper in a dead man's kitchen?"

"Are you sure you've never met him before?" Brownhill asked.

"The first time I set eyes on the bloke was five minutes before I phoned you lot."

Two paramedics came in with a stretcher.

"Sorry it's taken so long," one of them said to Grant Webber. "There was a massive pile-up on the A-19 and we've been run off our feet."

"No problem," Webber told him. "This one's past saving anyway."

The cold, lifeless body of Frank Broadbent was rolled onto the stretcher - the two paramedics covered him with a sheet and carried him out the door.

"There's not much more we can do here tonight," Brownhill said. "We're going to need to get a positive ID on him, but that can wait until tomorrow."

"I still have a few things to look at in here," Webber told her.

"Let's call it a night, then," Brownhill looked at Smith. "Can I have a word?"

"I don't know who he is," Smith told her when the rest of the team had left. "If I did I'd tell you."

"I believe you. That's not what I wanted to talk to you about. Great work on the fireworks bust. It looks like you've cleared a whole load of potentially deadly fireworks off the streets."

"It was Yang Chu who did most of the groundwork," Smith admitted. "He's the one who deserves a pat on the back."

"It was a textbook team effort. With you at the helm. Well done."

"Don't speak too soon. We've still got to interview the two scumbags involved. Their legal aid can't make it until tomorrow morning."

"The fireworks are out of harm's way," Brownhill said. "That's the main thing. I'll see you bright and early tomorrow."

* * *

Smith opened the door of his house and went inside. Theakston and Fred had heard the sound of his car door and were waiting for him in the hallway. The Bull Terrier and the Pug jumped up at Smith's legs and instantly lifted his spirits. He almost forgot about what had happened in the past hour or so.

Almost.

Whitton was feeding Laura in the kitchen. Smith walked through, kissed them both and took a beer out of the fridge. He sat down opposite his daughter and took a long swig out of the bottle.

"Rough day?" Whitton asked.

Smith told her about his discovery on Bartlett Street.

"And you think it was Frank Broadbent that phoned you this morning?" Whitton's eyes were wide.

"It looks like it," Smith replied. "But I still have no idea why. I've never met the man before in my life, so why would he have my phone number on a piece of paper in his kitchen?"

"And what's the story with the snake? A Black Mamba you say?"

"Its Latin name was written on the paper. It's baffling the crap out of me. I suppose we'll know more when we get cause of death. It looks like we've cleared up the fireworks investigation though. We caught two men with the whole stash. And you wouldn't believe who one of them was."

"Who?"

"The younger brother of the scumbag who mugged my Gran."

"You're joking? Although I suppose it's not unusual for crime to run in families."

"And the scumbag who mugged my Gran is no longer with us. He was stabbed outside a pub and didn't make it. Good riddance I say."

"Good riddance," Whitton agreed. "Are you hungry?"

"Not really," Smith replied. "I think I might just jump in the shower – wash the day off me, and go to bed. I've got a terrible feeling tomorrow is going to be a shitty day."

The sound of sirens could be heard in the distance as Smith stood under the warm jets of the shower.

Fire engines if he wasn't mistaken.

He let the water blast down onto his head and felt the weariness of the day wash away. He stood there until the water started to cool slightly, turned off the taps and dried himself. He brushed his teeth and climbed into bed, his hair still soaking wet.

CHAPTER THIRTEEN

Smith shot up in bed and opened his eyes wide. He was covered in sweat and he could hear his heart beating in his ears. He'd been dreaming about snakes – huge, thick green and black snakes, and something about the dream had made him wake up. He took a deep breath and tried to slow his heartbeat. He'd already forgotten what it was about the dream that had made him wake up so abruptly. He looked at the clock on the bedside table. It was 6:45. Whitton was breathing heavily next to him. Smith got out of bed, dressed and went downstairs.

It was not yet light as Smith opened up the back door and an icy gust of wind blew in. He closed the door immediately and decided his first cigarette of the day could wait. He made some coffee and sat down at the table. He wondered what the day had in store for him. Darren Maude and David Atkins would need to be interviewed, and Smith wasn't looking forward to it at all. Brownhill had commended him on a job well done, but Smith knew it was far from over. The fireworks were off the streets, but the only thing they could pin on Maude and Atkins was the fact that they had found stolen fireworks in Maude's back garden. It would be impossible to make a case for any of the injuries caused by the faulty fireworks. All Maude and Atkins had to do would be to deny everything, and Smith knew they had no real evidence to prove otherwise.

He picked up his phone and remembered it had died sometime yesterday and he had forgotten to charge it. He plugged it into the charger, waited a few moments then switched the phone on. He saw he'd missed eight calls and received four messages, two of them voice messages. He dialled his voicemail service and listened. The first one was from Brownhill.

"There's been a serious fire on King Street." The DI sounded anxious. "Number 47 to be precise. The fire brigade is already there, but it looks like all those fireworks have gone up in flames."

Smith listened to the message again. He couldn't believe it – a shed full of fireworks had exploded the same day they'd arrested two men suspected of stealing them.

That fire was no accident, he thought.

The second voice message was from Bridge basically elaborating on what Brownhill had told him. Darren Maude's shed had been totally destroyed. The adjacent house had suffered extensive fire damage. Apparently it had been quite a spectacle according to a number of eye witnesses. The text messages were both from the same number. It was a number Smith didn't recognise. Both of them consisted of the same four words.

Let the games begin.

Smith frowned, took a sip of coffee and put down the phone. He wasn't in the mood for cryptic text messages this early in the morning.

An hour later, the sun had come up and Smith was sat at his desk in his office. He opened up his emails. Dr Kenny Bean had sent him a copy of the initial path report for Frank Broadbent. Smith was surprised Dr Bean had managed to conduct a post mortem so quickly. Cause of death was suspected to be through respiratory failure, but the reason for the failure was still unknown. Rigor and Liver Mortis put the time of death at around mid-morning the previous day.

Respiratory failure? Smith thought and remembered how Frank Broadbent had been lying on the floor with his hands around his neck.

He couldn't breathe.

Smith took out his phone and dialled Kenny Bean's number. The pathologist with the bizarre sense of humour answered straight away.

"I assume you've read it, then?"

"I'm looking at the report now," Smith told him. "I just needed to ask you something."

"Shoot. I've got a meeting with the hospital directors in ten minutes but I wouldn't mind finding an excuse to miss it. Tedious bunch of vampires that lot."

Smith smiled. "The report states the cause of death was respiratory failure. Are you saying it was due to natural causes?"

"I'm saying no such thing. I go with the facts. Judging from the coloration of the poor bugger's skin, and the fact that the oxygen levels in his blood were incredibly low, it means his lungs couldn't keep the arterial oxygen at a safe enough level and he basically suffocated. Hypoxemia if you want to learn a new word today."

"Thanks, doc. When do you think you'll have something more for us?"

"I'm not sure if there is anything else to find. But later this afternoon if I make it a priority."

"It is a priority," Smith said. "Enjoy the meeting with the directors."

    Smith suddenly thought of something else. Something he should have asked Dr Bean straight away. He pressed redial on his mobile phone.

"Kenny, there was something else I needed to ask you."

"The board of directors can wait," Dr Bean said. "What is it?"

"Could Frank Broadbent have died due to a snake bite?"

"I think this phone line is bad. Did you just say snake bite?"

"Could the poison from a snake have caused the respiratory failure?"

"Theoretically, yes," the pathologist replied. "But not from the poison from any snake native to these parts. In fact we've only got one venomous snake in the UK – the adder – and, as far as I'm aware there have been no fatalities in years. Its venom isn't potent enough to cause any concern to human beings."

"What about a Black Mamba?"

"I think you need more sleep, detective. A Mamba wouldn't last five minutes in our climate. Their natural habitat is Sub-Saharan Africa."

"I didn't ask if we have Black Mambas slithering around on the moors," Smith said. "Could the venom from a Black Mamba cause the symptoms Frank Broadbent had?"

"I'm by no means an expert, but I understand the venom from a Black Mamba is predominantly neurotoxic which could account for the respiratory paralysis and eventual cardiovascular collapse, but I think you're barking up the wrong tree here. And I'm late for that meeting."

"Is there any way you could check?" Smith wasn't giving up. "Check for the poison in his system? And any bite marks. I would really appreciate it."

Dr Bean sighed. "I'll get onto it as soon as the meeting is finished. Goodbye, Detective Smith."

CHAPTER FOURTEEN

Smith left his office and headed for the canteen. Bridge and Yang Chu were drinking coffee by the window. Smith sat down at their table.

"Where were you last night?" Bridge asked him.

"Where I ought to be most nights," Smith replied. "At home with my family."

"We tried to get hold of you."

"My phone died. I forgot to charge it."

"I suppose you heard about the fire on King Street?" Yang Chu said.

"I got Bridge's and the DI's messages this morning. Do we know what happened yet?"

"I reckon Darren Maude called someone from in here and got them to torch the shed," Bridge theorized.

"Why?" Smith said. "Why would he want to burn down his shed, and risk setting fire to his house at the same time?"

"To get rid of the evidence of course," Bridge said.

"We've got enough evidence. Webber went over the place thoroughly. He's got photos of the fireworks – the boxes had serial numbers on them. We know they were the same ones that were stolen from the container in Hull. We caught them red-handed yesterday. We've got more than enough to nail them for handling stolen goods and selling illegal fireworks. Do you know what time legal aid are going to get here?"

"They're on the way," Yang Chu said. "Brownhill wants me and her to interview both Darren Maude and David Atkins. Is that OK with you?"

"She's the boss. There is one thing though. Something that's been bugging me, and something you need to bring up in the interviews."

"What's that?"

"How did they know?" Smith said. "How did they know about the container full of condemned fireworks in the first place? Hull is about forty miles away isn't it? I very much doubt scumbags like Maude and Atkins have contacts in Customs and Excise, so I think someone else is involved."

"I'll ask the DI about bringing it up. Anything else?"

"Good luck – it'll be good experience for you. I'm going for a drive."

"Where are you going?" Bridge asked.

"To irritate a bad-tempered forensics officer."

Smith drove out of the car park at the station. The more he thought about the conversation he'd had with Dr Kenny Bean, the more what he had said made sense. They hadn't seen any reason to connect the hand-written note with Smith's mobile number on it to the death of Frank Broadbent. But now they were armed with the initial pathology report Smith knew they had to take it seriously. The Latin name of a deadly snake was written on the note, and the way Frank Broadbent had died could have been caused by the venom from that snake.

Grant Webber was examining something on a laptop in his lab when Smith came in. He was so engrossed in whatever it was he didn't even hear Smith until he was standing right behind him. Smith looked closely at the screen.

"What are we looking at?"

"DS Smith," Webber didn't turn around. "There are only two explanations why you should be here in person, and they both usually mean a headache for me."

"Two reasons?" Smith was intrigued.

"You either want me to prioritise something or you have something else you need me to look at. Either of the two has the effect of buggering up my day. What do you want?"

Smith looked at the image on the screen. "Is that the weird contraption we found at Frank Broadbent's house?"

"It is. I've never seen anything like it before."

"Do you know what it is?"

"The base is metal. Aluminium, I think. Light weight. And the spring and wire are probably stainless steel. Much stronger. It appears to work on the same concept as a mousetrap – the spring is pulled back and held under tension by the wire, but it's this thin tube that has me baffled. The only explanation I can give for its design is to act like a syringe, albeit an incredibly minute one."

"Any fingerprints?"

"That's the odd thing. None whatsoever. It appears to be handmade so one would expect to find something, even if it's just a partial but this was clean."

"What about on the envelope or the note that I found on the floor?"

"Plenty on the envelope, but that's not unusual considering it's been through the postal system. There were a couple on the paper, but we haven't had a chance to get to them yet."

"How much do you know about snakes?" Smith asked out of the blue.

"Not much," Webber admitted. "Apart from knowing I'm not particularly fond of cold blooded creatures. Why do you ask?"

Smith told him about his conversation with Kenny Bean. Webber listened intently.

"Hmm," the head of forensics said when Smith was finished. He got up from his chair. "I want you to have a look at something."

Smith followed him down a corridor to another lab. Two of Webber's team were working on something at a large desk. Webber stopped next to them. On the desk was the odd metal contraption they'd found in Frank Broadbent's kitchen. Webber donned a pair of gloves and took out some tiny tweezers. He picked up the thin metal tube and held it in front of his face.

"Harry," he said to a man Smith had never met before. "Assemble the device like you did earlier."

Harry did as he was asked. When he was finished, the spring on the mousetrap-like contraption was tensioned and held by the wire. Webber carefully attached the thin metal tube with the even thinner needle inside. "What do you think it is?" he asked Smith.

Smith studied it carefully. He'd never had a scientific brain, but a picture was forming in his head of what they were actually looking at.

"If it was taped inside the envelope," he said. "And the wire itself was taped to the part of the envelope where it says, 'OPEN HERE' the opener of the envelope would activate the spring and the needle would shoot out."

"What exactly are you saying?"

"That what you have on your desk is a very ingenious letter bomb," Smith told him. "And I would handle it very carefully from now on. If I'm not mistaken that needle will still have traces of one of the deadliest snake venoms there are on it."

CHAPTER FIFTEEN

"Where have you been?" DI Brownhill was standing by the front desk when Smith walked in.

"Good morning to you too, boss," Smith said. "I've been spending some quality time with your man, Grant. We seem to be getting on like a house on fire these days. We really must do dinner together sometime."

"Not likely. You've found something haven't you? I know that smug grin."

"I was born with it, boss. I think I know what happened to Frank Broadbent."

He told her his suspicions about the elaborate letter bomb.

"A letter bomb that injects snake venom into the victim?" Brownhill didn't sound very convinced. "That's a bit far-fetched isn't it?"

"Very," Smith agreed. "I've asked Kenny Bean to check for traces of the poison in Frank Broadbent, and Webber is doing the same with the needle we found. It's going to take a while, but at least we'll know for sure."

"You've come up with some wild theories in the past, Smith but this one has to take the biscuit."

"We'll see. How did the interviews with the Guy Fawkes thieves go?"

"As well as could be expected. And please don't call them that? Both Maude and Atkins denied any involvement in the fire."

"They would, wouldn't they?"

"The only phone calls either of them made were to their legal representatives. And their appointed solicitors confirmed this. As far as we could tell the news about the fire came as a total surprise to them."

"Did you ask them how they knew about the container in Hull in the first place?"

"Yang Chu did pass on your suggestion, yes. Darren Maude claimed to have heard it on the grapevine in the pub, and David Atkins denied all knowledge of it. He was just the middleman so to speak."

"And who actually stole the fireworks?"

"Neither of them would tell us."

"No offence, boss, but I think you're losing your touch. Do you want me and Bridge to have another crack at them?"

"It won't help," Brownhill looked more hurt than angry. "We have enough to charge them with dealing in stolen goods – the fireworks have been disposed of, albeit in a rather unorthodox manner and as far as we're concerned this matter is closed."

"It's far from closed," Smith realised he'd raised his voice. "This stinks of an inside job. Someone in Customs or someone who works at that container port was in on it, and who's to say another dodgy shipment of fireworks won't arrive anytime soon?"

"I don't know how many resources you think we have at our disposal, DS Smith," Brownhill was clearly angry now. "But we are facing more and more cutbacks every year. We cannot simply throw everything we have into a long drawn out investigation that will probably lead nowhere. I will say this for the last time. This matter is closed."

Smith slammed the door to his office behind him and sat down behind his desk. He couldn't understand why he had got so angry with Brownhill. He knew the DI was right – an investigation into corruption in Customs and Excise would be a costly affair, and there was no way the powers that be would authorise it. He tried to think realistically. The fireworks were off the streets, two low-life criminals would also be off the streets for a while, and as far as Superintendent Smyth's crime stats were concerned this case was considered cleared up.

But Smith was still furious. Whitton had always told him he took things far too personally, and some things were out of his control. He'd always envied her stoicism. She had explained it to him once.

Yorkshire stoicism. Her father was a firm believer in it.

If you can change it – do it, but if there's nowt you can do about it, don't waste time worrying about it.

Smith knew it was never going to be a philosophy he'd be able to adopt.

The ringtone on his phone interrupted his thoughts. He looked at the screen and saw it was Dr Kenny Bean.

"That was quick," Smith said.

"The meeting was cancelled," Dr Bean told him. "Half of those due at the meeting are sick in bed with flu. Rather ironic wouldn't you agree? We're unable to hold a hospital directors' meeting because half of them are off sick."

"Have you found something?"

"Indeed I have. But I'd rather not discuss it over the phone – you'd better come to the hospital. And I hope your flu jab is up to date – they're dropping like flies in here."

Smith drove far too quickly to the hospital on the other side of town. He'd known Kenny Bean for some years now and he knew the head of pathology was not one to waste his time calling him in to the hospital unless he had a very good reason.

Smith parked as close to the entrance as possible. He got out of the car and smiled when something Whitton had said came back to him. She'd mentioned that Smith had spent so much time in this hospital he ought to have his own designated parking place by now.

He found Dr Bean in his office.

"Take a seat," he said.

Smith sat opposite him. "Tell me you've found something."

"You were lucky. These kinds of tests generally take some time, but I happen to be fortunate enough to have a pathologist on my team who happens to lean towards the weirder end of the human spectrum."

"Just the one?"

"Do you want to hear what I've got for you or not?"

"Sorry," Smith said. "Go on."

"Dr Lillian Marx is considered quite an authority in the field of Herpetology. That's reptiles to people like you and I. She is especially expert in venomous asps. She spent many years in Africa and Asia studying these heinous creatures, and her research was mostly in the interest of producing anti-venom more economically than it had been produced in the past."

Dr Bean looked Smith in the eyes.

"Please go on," Smith urged.

"What Lillian found is far from conclusive," Dr Bean continued. "But as she already knew what we were looking for, her job was made somewhat easier. Your dead man did have what could be Black Mamba venom in his system."

"Could be?"

"In pathology we like to be exact. When I say Lillian's findings are far from conclusive I mean she's 95 percent positive."

"Seventy-five would have been good enough for me."

"The venom of the Black Mamba is rather unique amongst snake species in that it doesn't contain any protease enzymes and therefore its bite rarely causes any local swelling or necrosis. And that unfortunately brings me to my next point. We could find nothing to suggest the victim received any kind of bite. There were no puncture wounds anywhere on the body that resembled a snake bite."

"He wasn't bitten by the snake," Smith told him.

"The plot thickens, does it?"

Smith told him everything from the beginning. How he'd stumbled upon Frank Broadbent's body simply by accident, how he'd discovered the note mentioning the Black Mamba, and what he'd deduced from Webber's analysis of the metal contraption found on the kitchen table.

"A venomous letter bomb?" Dr Bean exclaimed. "How original."

There wasn't a hint of sarcasm in his voice.

"Has Webber not sent the needle here for testing?" Smith asked.

"We received it a few hours ago, but Grant isn't anywhere near as persistent nor *insistent* as you, DS Smith. In fact, when The Ghoul told me about you before his untimely demise, I thought he was exaggerating. Nobody could possibly be that annoyingly assiduous. Of course, now I know better. I'll have Dr Marx have a look at it right away."

"How come I haven't seen this Dr Marx before? I know most of your team."

"Lillian only recently arrived," Dr Bean told him. "She's just finished a two year stint in your old stomping ground actually."

"Australia?"

"In case you've forgotten, Oz has some rather nasty poisonous critters. We'd better get started with that needle Webber sent over."

"You will find Black Mamba Venom on that needle," Smith insisted.

"No doubt we will," Dr Bean mused. "No doubt we will."

CHAPTER SIXTEEN

Smith realised straight away that Dr Bean's findings had put a whole new perspective on the death of Frank Broadbent. They were now looking at a murder and a particularly well planned and carefully thought-out one at that. He'd already pushed the fireworks episode out of his mind – compared to this, a missing consignment of faulty fireworks was not even worth worrying about. Kenny Bean had promised to prioritise the needle and told Smith he would have the results back within the hour.

Smith knocked on Brownhill's office door and opened it. The DI was reading something on her desk.

"I was right," Smith told her.

Brownhill looked up at him. "Of course you were. What were you right about?"

"Kenny Bean has a snake specialist working with him. She's confirmed Frank Broadbent had Black Mamba venom in his system, and in less than an hour she's going to confirm that she's found the same venom on the needle of the device that was used to inject Mr Broadbent. We've got a murder to investigate. This was a carefully planned murder."

"OK," Brownhill said. "What are your initial thoughts?"

"I don't have any," Smith admitted. "Why go to such great lengths to kill someone? I've never seen anything like it before. And that note we found is just bizarre. Somebody got hold of my mobile number and wrote it at the bottom. Why would somebody do that?"

"Somebody who doesn't like you?" Brownhill suggested.

"Lots of people don't like me, but it still doesn't make any sense. You need to call a briefing as soon as possible."

"Until we get confirmation that there was poison on that needle, I'm not calling anything. Wait and see what Kenny's expert has to say and we'll take it from there."

Forty five minutes later Dr Lillian Marx called Smith personally to inform him of two things : Firstly, she'd found minute traces of Black Mamba venom on the needle Webber had sent, and secondly, if the tube the needle was inserted into had been full of the poison, Frank Broadbent wouldn't have stood a chance. The dosage was just too high. The fast-working neurotoxic venom would have probably stopped his heart within an hour.

Smith found Brownhill in the canteen and told her the news.

"Where is everybody else?" he asked. "I can't find Bridge or Yang Chu anywhere."

"The last time I saw Bridge he was in his office. And Yang Chu is busy with the report on the fireworks case. Speak of the devils."

Bridge and Yang Chu came in together. Both of them had smiles on their faces.

"You two are in a good mood," Smith said. "We'll soon put an end to that. We've just found out that Frank Broadbent was murdered."

"Murdered?" Yang Chu repeated.

"In a most ingenious way," Smith added.

Brownhill filled them in on what they knew so far.

"Bloody hell," Bridge said afterwards. "What a horrible way to die. Fighting for breath like that. So, now we need to look into Frankie Boy's history. Find out if anyone could possibly want him dead."

"Don't call him that," Brownhill said. "As far as we know Frank Broadbent was thirty-six-years old. Single, no children. He'd worked as a manager for a restaurant in town for two years and before that he spent ten years with the Post Office. We're going to need to speak to everybody who knew him – family, friends, work colleagues. As is usual during this stage of an investigation we have more questions than answers. There will be a formal briefing at four this afternoon, but in the meantime does anybody have any suggestions regarding any other questions we need to be asking ourselves?"

"The note," Bridge said. "What was that all about?"

"Sick joke?" Yang Chu suggested.

"Very sick if you ask me," Bridge agreed. "Claiming the poor bastard had won a prize. That is some perverted mind."

"Where did the poison come from?" Smith said and everybody turned to look at him. "Surely Black Mamba venom isn't readily available? How did the killer get hold of it?"

"All good questions," Brownhill said. "And ones we will address at the briefing."

"Can I make a suggestion, boss?" Smith said.

"Of course."

"We can go through the motions like we always do – look more closely at the victim, follow up on the evidence we have, but I think we're going to need a bit of outside help with this one."

"I don't like the sound of this. It sounds like it could be expensive."

"Not at all. This expert of Kenny Bean's is a whizz with snakes. I say we bring her in, in an advisory capacity. I'll speak to Kenny – it won't cost the York Police a penny."

"I'll give it some thought."

"Dr Marx has worked with snakes all over the world," Smith carried on unperturbed. "She's been involved in the development of anti-venom for years, and if anybody knows where to get hold of snake poison, she does."

"Smith's got a point, Ma'am," Bridge said.

"What harm can it do?" Yang Chu joined in. "Especially if it's not going to cost us anything."

"I said I'll give it some thought. Now, we still have a few hours before the briefing, so I suggest we use that time to gather as much information about Mr Frank Broadbent as possible."

CHAPTER SEVENTEEN

Lofthouse's was a relatively new addition to York's restaurant scene. The family-themed restaurant and pub franchise had been the brainchild of Greg Lofthouse – a retired football player who'd found a passion for the restaurant industry around five years earlier. Greg had been well advised and, unlike many other retired sportsmen had invested his savings wisely. Five years on and there were now over twenty Lofthouse's dotted around the country.

"This is your kind of place, Sarge," Yang Chu said to Smith outside.
"What on earth are you talking about?" Smith asked.
"Family pub. Play area for the kids. Now you have a young daughter I mean."
"There's nothing wrong with the beer garden at the Hog's Head. I've never liked these places."
"It's simple economics isn't it? Keep the kids happy and entertained and the parents stick around and spend more money."
"Wise words, Yang Chu."

They had arranged to meet Tommy Bonner, the owner of the York franchise. Brownhill had warned them about disclosing too much information – if the bit about the Black Mamba got out the press would have a field day, but Tommy Bonner was ex-job, and an old friend of Chalmers and the DCI had ensured them that nothing they told him would go any further. The place was empty when Smith and Yang Chu walked in. Smith was amazed at how clean the restaurant was. The bar area was small, and it struck him straight away this wasn't a place to come for a few drinks after work.

A tall, balding man with a friendly face approached them. He walked with a slight limp. He looked Smith up and down and then held out his hand. "You must be from the police. Tommy Bonner. We can talk in my office."

Smith didn't normally like shaking hands with other men, but as this was an old friend of Chalmers' he made an exception. They walked past the empty tables and chairs and Tommy led them up a glass staircase to where his office was situated. He opened the door and gestured for them to go inside. "Take a seat. Can I offer you something to drink?"

Smith felt like a beer. He felt like more than one beer.

"Coffee would be great," he said.

Tommy Bonner walked over to his desk, pressed a button on a rather complicated-looking telephone. "Janet, could you whip up three coffees for us please?"

"I still can't believe Frank is dead," Tommy closed the door and sat opposite Smith and Yang Chu. "It doesn't seem real. I'm no spring chicken – I was in the job for thirty years, so I'm no stranger to death but it still knocks you for a six each time. He was fighting fit on Sunday. We had a birthday party in. Sixty kids and Frank handled it like it was six. He seemed fine on Sunday."

"Mr Bonner," Smith said. "How well did you know Mr Broadbent?"

"Please, call me Tommy. I've known Frank for two years. He made an impression on me if that's the right way to put it. He applied for the job of restaurant manager without a scrap of experience to his name. He worked for the Post Office before then if I can recall. But he had something. Something that experience can't teach you, I saw the potential – took a chance on him and he never let me down in the two years he was here."

"Can you think of anybody who would want to hurt him? Do you know if Mr Broadbent had any enemies?"

"Of course not. Frank was a likeable bloke. Kept himself to himself most of the time. Hold on, are you saying somebody did this to him? Somebody killed him."

"We're not ruling anything out at the moment," Yang Chu got in first with the old police cliché.

Tommy Bonner laughed. "That old chestnut. I haven't heard that in years. I miss the job sometimes."

"Where were you based?" Smith asked him.

"Leeds. I rose up the ranks to detective inspector and I decided that's where I wanted to stay."

"Sounds familiar."

"I'd still be there if it wasn't for the old knee. Some wise-arse seemed to take exception to it and went at it with a baseball bat. I was offered early retirement and I took it. I used the pay-out to buy into this place."

"Tommy," Smith continued. "As far as you're aware was Mr Broadbent involved with anyone? Girlfriend?"

"Not that I knew of, but like I said, Frank kept himself to himself and it's not really any of my business is it? What exactly happened to him?"

Smith thought hard. He was usually very good with first impressions and Tommy Bonner had made a particularly good one on him. Besides, he was an ex-detective and an old friend of Chalmers' to boot so that meant he was probably someone he could trust.

"Tommy, what I'm about to tell you is to stay within these four walls. Do you understand?"

"Of course," Tommy looked at him curiously. "I know the drill."

"My boss said as much."

"How is Bob? I must make some time to pay him a visit. I haven't had time to breathe since I took over the franchise. This business takes up most of my time."

"Bob's still the same," Smith replied and realised Chalmers' first name sounded rather odd coming out of his mouth.

There was a knock on the door, it was opened and a woman in her early twenties came in with a tray of coffee.

"Thank you, Janet," Tommy said.

She nodded, turned around and left the room.

Tommy poured the coffee. "Go on. You've got me rather intrigued. What were you about to say?"

"Like I said," Smith said. "This information cannot get out. We believe Mr Broadbent was murdered."

"Murdered? Why? How?"

"We're still working on that, but our initial findings lead us to believe some kind of elaborate letter bomb was used."

"A bomb?" Tommy's eyes widened. "Like a terrorist attack?"

"Nothing quite so dramatic. Mr Broadbent was the victim of a letter that when he opened it a needle shot out and injected him with poison. We believe he died in under an hour."

"This is unbelievable. What kind of poison could do that?"

"Snake poison," Yang Chu told him.

"A Black Mamba," Smith elaborated. "We're not normally in the habit of divulging such information, but it could be that the way Mr Broadbent was killed may have something to do with the man himself. Do you know if he had any interest in exotic snakes?"

"Not that I'm aware of. Are you sure it was the poison from a Black Mamba?"

"Positive. An expert in the field has confirmed it."

"And do you know where a person might be able to get their hands on Black Mamba poison?"

Smith smiled. "We'll be looking into it."

"Sorry. Once a detective always a detective."

Tommy Bonner's phone started to ring on his desk.

"Excuse me," he looked at Smith. "I'd better take this."

Smith looked around the room. It was far too modern for his liking but the huge glass windows afforded an impressive view of the whole city. He concluded that family restaurant franchises were rather lucrative businesses to be in. A noise behind him made him turn around. It sounded like soft footsteps. The noise was coming from behind the closed door of the office. Tommy replaced the phone. "Sorry to cut short the chat, but I'm wanted downstairs. We're a bit short staffed without Frank, and there's a paranoid mother who's not sure if this place is child-friendly enough for a birthday party for a load of four-year-olds."

"This must be a far cry from being a DI in Leeds," Yang Chu said.

"It has its moments."

"Thank you for your time, Tommy." Smith handed him one of his cards. "If you think of anything else give me a call."

"Will do. And give my regards to Bob. Tell him I'll be in touch."

CHAPTER EIGHTEEN

Smith and Yang Chu arrived back at the station with fifteen minutes to spare before the four o clock briefing so they headed for their usual pre-briefing place. Brownhill and Bridge were deep in discussion at the table next to the complicated coffee machine. Smith got a strong coffee and stood at their table.

"Anything new come up?" he addressed them both.

"We spoke with Frank Broadbent's sister," Bridge told him. "They weren't that close, but she's upset. According to her, Frank was quite a boring man."

"Boring?" Smith repeated.

"That's what she reckons. All he ever wanted to do was go to work and come home and repeat the process. He was never really interested in anything. No girlfriends that she can remember and no hobbies."

"What a life," Smith said. "What about friends?"

"Didn't you hear what I just said? Frank Broadbent didn't have a life."

"That's really depressing. And now he's dead."

"We'll have a guest at the meeting," Brownhill said. "I've spoken to Grant, and also to Kenny Bean and they both agree that Dr Lillian Marx's input could be valuable. She will be acting in an independent advisory role and she has offered her services free of charge."

"Isn't that what I said this morning, boss?" Smith said.

"And I decided to agree with you."

"Are we on the same page again? This has got to stop – people are going to start talking."

"That's enough. Finish your coffee. Let's make a start, shall we?"

* * *

The first thing Smith noticed when he walked into the small conference room was how cold it was in there. DCI Chalmers was already seated at the table.

Smith sat down next to him. "How did you manage to escape the Super?"

"Smyth is in conference with the Chief Constable," Chalmers told him. "Something about his crime stats presentation next month. I was supposed to be there, but I managed to pull the wool over the public-school buffoon's eyes. I told him the crime stats thing was his baby and only his. And that the Chief would only want to his input so I was surplus to requirements."

"And he bought that?"

"What do you think?"

"Why is it so cold in here today?" Smith asked.

"The radiator's buggered. There was someone supposed to come and look at it, but you know what it's like. It could take them weeks."

"Let's get started, shall we." It was Brownhill. "Smith, you're heading this one up. What have we got so far?"

"Frank Broadbent was found yesterday afternoon," Smith started from the beginning. "Acting on a tip-off from Mr Broadbent's employer I went to his house and found him on the floor in his kitchen. He was dead. We've since discovered the cause of death was the venom from a particularly poisonous snake – the Black Mamba. We also now know how Mr Broadbent ended up with snake venom in his system. An elaborate letter-bomb-like contraption was found in his kitchen, and the needle on that device had traces of the same venom on it."

The door opened and a woman who appeared to be in her mid-thirties came in. She was tall and athletically-built with mousy-blonde hair tied up in a tight ponytail. She was wearing jeans, a green jumper and a padded jacket. Everyone turned to look at her. Bridge seemed to take a very keen interest in her.

"Sorry I'm late," she spoke with an odd accent. "The battery in my car died. It's this cold weather."

"Doctor Marx?" Brownhill asked.

"That's me." She took a seat next to the DI. "Have I missed anything?"

"DS Smith was just filling us in on what we have so far. I believe you already know most of it anyway."

Dr Marx zipped up her jacket as far as it would go. "Is it always so cold in here?"

"Heater's knackered," Bridge told her and smiled. "Someone's supposed to be coming out to fix it."

"Can we continue?" Brownhill urged. She nodded to Smith.

"The device that was used to inject Frank Broadbent was concealed in an A4 envelope. It was designed in such a way that as soon as he opened the envelope the spring was released and the needle shot out. We've got nothing from the envelope – it was sent through the post so there were prints all over it. The address on the front was handwritten in block capitals, as was the note that was inside."

"Note?" this was clearly news to Dr Marx.

"Yang Chu," Smith said.

DC Yang Chu switched on the projector, typed a few keys on a laptop and an image appeared on the large screen.

'CONGRATULATIONS. YOU HAVE BEEN CHOSEN TO RECEIVE A SPECIAL PRIZE – A GIFT FROM A DENDROAPSIS POLYLEPIS. YOUR REWARD IS OBLIVION. SHOULD YOU DECIDE NOT TO ACCEPT THIS PRIZE, PHONE THE NUMBER BELOW AND REPEAT THESE FOUR SIMPLE WORDS – I WANT TO LIVE.'

"That's what was in the envelope," Smith said.

"Dendroapsis Polyepsis," Dr Marx read. "Black Mamba."

"That's right," Brownhill said. "Very nasty snake, by all accounts."

"That depends on what you mean by nasty," Dr Marx said and everyone in the room turned to look at her. "If you mean that if you encroach upon its territory expect to suffer the consequences. A Black Mamba will not hesitate to strike if it feels threatened, but most of the time it will keep out of your way. Any animal will instinctively protect its territory, and we as human beings are not exempt to this."

"Where is that accent from?" Smith asked in an attempt to steer the conversation in another direction.

"All over the place," Dr Marx's facial features appeared to relax slightly. "I'm a bit of a fake – a chameleon really, and I tend to pick up on accents wherever I end up. Who knows, after a few months in Yorkshire I may even end up saying things like *nowt* and *over yonder*."

Bridge started to laugh. Brownhill glared at him.

"Dr Marx," the DI said. "We've asked you to join us as an advisor and we are very grateful for your input. The first thing you can help us with is this. Where would one obtain the venom from a snake such as a Black Mamba?"

"On the black market," Dr Marx replied without hesitation. "And definitely not in this country."

"How do you know that?" Brownhill asked.

"There is no reason whatsoever for anyone to possess Black Mamba venom in the UK. Its only use is to render somebody paralysed then, inevitably dead."

"What about for making anti-venom?" Bridge suggested.

Dr Marx rolled her eyes. "As far as I know there have been no recorded Mamba bites in this country – and I don't know how much you know about anti-venom, but you don't just pick up a bit of snake poison, then Google how to turn it into anti-venom. No, this venom was bought overseas."

"What about milking?" Chalmers joined in. "Couldn't the venom have come from someone with a Black Mamba who obtained the poison through milking it?"

"The only Black Mambas I'm aware of in this country are kept in snake parks and zoos. It is highly illegal to keep that species of snake as a pet, and what sane person would want a Mamba as a pet anyway?"

"We're talking about a murderer," Smith reminded her. "They're generally not the sanest members of society."

"OK," Brownhill could sense the mood in the small conference room was beginning to mirror the temperature inside. "It gives us something to look into. What do we know about the victim?"

"We spoke to his boss," Smith said. "And according to him, Frank Broadbent was the model employee. Always gave a hundred percent, never late for work."

"It was Tommy Bonner, his employer who tipped us off about Mr Broadbent's absence," Chalmers said.

"Luckily he did," Bridge said. "Otherwise he could still be lying on the floor in his kitchen."

"Anything else?" Brownhill said.

"He was a bit of a nobody according to his sister," Bridge said. "No friends, no ambition. All he wanted out of life was a job and financial security."

"About that," Baldwin spoke for the first time. "I don't think we should ignore the correspondence we found. He owed a mail-order catalogue money and there was a final reminder from the gas board."

"I don't believe that has any relevance in this, Baldwin," Smith said and rubbed his eyes. "The man owed less than six hundred quid, and I think the gas board just cut you off – they don't inject you with deadly snake venom."

"Does anybody have anything constructive to add?" Brownhill said in a stern voice.

"My mobile phone number," Smith thought out loud. "Why was it that Frank Broadbent was told to call my phone number?"

The room was silent. Smith noticed that Bridge was staring at Dr Lillian Marx. He was not being very subtle about it.

"I've never met the man," Smith broke the silence after a few seconds. "Why would whoever killed him leave my number for him to call?"

"What if." Chalmers said. "What if *you've* never met the victim, but the killer has met *you*?"

CHAPTER NINETEEN

"The DCI suggested you've met the killer?" Whitton said.

Smith was halfway through his third beer. They were sitting in their living room, the television was on and Laura was sitting on a blanket, captivated by a documentary about dolphins.

"When you think about it, it does make sense," Smith finished the beer in one large gulp. "It's not like someone has just plucked a number out of thin air. Whoever is responsible for this would know I would be involved in the investigation."

"But why?" Whitton asked.

"I really have no idea. I've got a sudden feeling of déjà vu. Remember Jimmy Fulton?"

Jimmy Fulton was responsible for more pain in Smith's life than anyone else. For weeks he tortured Smith with brutal murders that mirrored tragic events in Smith's life. It culminated in Jimmy Fulton killing Lucy McLean. Besides Whitton, Lucy was the only woman Smith had ever truly loved.

"There has to be some other explanation," Whitton said. "It's a rather elaborate way of getting to you don't you think?"

"Everything about this murder is elaborate. The rigged envelope – the perfectly engineered murder weapon, and the Black Mamba venom. It's not only elaborate, it's bordering on genius when you think about it."

"I wouldn't go that far."

"Think about it, Whitton. We've got a murder where the killer isn't even at the scene when the murder happens. There are no witnesses to worry about, and the note is so confusing that even if the victim does figure out what's happening, it's too late. This is as close as it gets to the perfect murder."

"What about the stamp on the envelope?" Whitton wasn't giving up yet.

"We looked at that. It was posted in Ripon. Anybody can jump in the car, drive for an hour and find a post box. It's irrelevant where the package was posted."

"Can we talk about something else?" Whitton said. "I'm back at work tomorrow and I'd quite like to enjoy the rest of my last day off."

Smith stood up. "Sorry. I'm going outside for a smoke. Can I get you a beer?"

"A cup of coffee would be great."

Theakston and Fred were waiting by the back door begging to go outside. Smith switched on the kettle, picked up his cigarettes and opened the door. Both dogs barged past him and went outside. Smith followed them out and lit a cigarette. The air outside was so crisp and clear that it froze his throat when he breathed in. The smoke he inhaled didn't do much to help. The two dogs did whatever they needed to do as quickly as possible and ran back inside the house. Smith closed the door behind them and gazed up at the sky. He'd never seen so many stars before – there were no clouds to be seen and for the first time in years Smith spotted what he believed was the Milky Way. He gazed up at the millions of stars for so long that by the time he put his cigarette to his mouth to take another drag it had gone out and his hands were numb. He threw the cigarette into the next-door-neighbour's garden, smiled at what he had just done and went back inside the house.

Smith put the coffee on the table and sat down next to her. He placed his hand on the back of her neck and she flinched.

"You're freezing," she said.

"You should see the stars outside. I've never seen anything like it. It's amazing how clear they are millions of miles away."

"Are you trying to be romantic?"

"God, no. Do I sound romantic?"

"A bit. I think you've been spending too much time with Bridge."

"I'm nothing like Bridge."

"I should hope so."

"Bridge is in love again," Smith told her and took a sip of his beer.

"When is Bridge not in love?"

"He's got it bad for one of Kenny Bean's team."

"He's in love with a pathologist?"

"She's also a snake freak. Doctor Lillian Marx. She's helping us out with the investigation."

"Really?" Whitton seemed surprised. "What's she like?"

"You don't like her."

"How can you say that? I haven't even met her."

"When have you ever liked any woman who's joined the team?"

"I have. It just takes me a while sometimes. What's she like?"

"Weird," was the first word that slipped off Smith's tongue. "She likes to play with snakes. She's only just joined Kenny Bean's team. Before that she worked all over the world developing new anti-venoms. She's been in Africa, India and she's just come back from a couple of years in Australia."

"It sounds like fascinating work," Whitton said.

"No it doesn't. I haven't told you this but I really don't like snakes."

"Isn't the place you were born full of them?"

"Exactly. So I know a bit about snakes. They're cold-blooded unemotional reptiles. Why anybody would want to keep a snake as a pet is beyond me. What's wrong with a dog?"

"I've never been scared of snakes," Whitton said. "When I was a kid I remember some animal guy brought a load of different animals to my school. There was a four foot long python. I was one of the only kids who dared to pick it up."

"Is there anything you're afraid of?"

"Not really," Whitton thought for a second. "Apart from romantic blokes."

Smith slapped her on the shoulder. "I need another beer."

Laura was now fast asleep on her blanket.

"I'm going to put that little lady to bed," Whitton said.

She picked Laura up, wrapped the blanket around her and carried her upstairs.

Smith opened the fridge and took out a bottle of beer. His mobile phone bleeped on the table to indicate he'd received a text message. He picked it up and opened up the message. It was from the same number he'd received a message from that morning and it was also rather cryptic.

The rules of the game are about to change.

Smith could feel his face reddening and his jaw muscles clenched. He decided he would reply to the message, but he couldn't think of anything to say. He typed in *Arsehole*, and pressed send.

"How do you block someone on your phone?" he asked Whitton in the living room.

"Who do you want to block?"

"I have no idea. Some idiot keeps sending me stupid messages."

He handed her the phone.

"Let the games begin," Whitton read. "The rules of the game are about to change?"

"How do I block the sender?"

"You click the three dots at the top and it gives you the option to block them. But I'd wait if I were you."

"What for?" Smith asked. "It's getting really annoying."

"Because you received the first one after Frank Broadbent was found dead. And after what Chalmers said about the killer knowing you it could be important. We can get the number checked out tomorrow. This could be a crucial lead."

"You could be right. Stranger things have happened."

"Have your hands defrosted yet?" Whitton asked.

"What?"

"If your hands have warmed up, a massage would be nice right now."

Smith put down his beer and began rubbing the back of her neck. "Not too cold for you?"

"Much better."

Smith increased the pressure slightly and Whitton closed her eyes.

"Do you think Laura would like a brother or sister?" she asked.

"I hadn't thought about it. Do you?"

"I don't really know, but it doesn't hurt to practice just in case does it?"

"Mrs Smith," Smith moved his hands away from her neck and kissed it. "We have a little lady asleep upstairs."

"And if I know that little lady she'll be asleep for another eight hours."

She turned around and kissed Smith on the lips. "You taste of beer."

"I thought you liked beer."

"I do," Whitton said, flung her arms round him and kissed him even harder.

CHAPTER TWENTY

Morgan Russell was late. It was becoming a regular occurrence, and he knew his boss at the supermarket where he worked as manager wouldn't tolerate it for much longer. His shift at the Sunshine Supermarket was due to start in twenty minutes – Morgan's son, Mark wasn't even dressed for school yet, and neither of them had eaten breakfast. Morgan looked at his watch for the third time in as many minutes and frowned.

"Mark," he shouted upstairs. "Get your backside down here right now."

A young boy sauntered down the stairs. Mark was ten years old – he was generally a good child, but he had no concept of time whatsoever.

Morgan had been divorced for nine months. The split had been an amicable one – mostly for the sake of their son, and as Morgan's ex-wife, Jane knew she was to marry a rather wealthy man after the divorce was finalised, Morgan had been allowed to keep the house. The only condition was he would look after Mark during the school term and Jane would have him on some weekends and holidays.

The agreement wasn't working out too well for Morgan Russell.

"I'm late for work," he told his son. "You'll have to make your own way to school."

"Dad," Mark said in a way only a boy who is not far away from his teens can say. "I'm ten. I'm allowed to walk to school on my own now."

"Your mother doesn't like it."

"We won't tell her then."

Morgan looked at his watch once more. It was 8:30. His shift at the supermarket had already started.

"Have you got your key?" he asked Mark.

"I'm not a kid, Dad. Go to work. I'll make myself some breakfast before school."

Morgan opened the front door and a blast of icy wind blew in.

"Wrap yourself up warm. And remember. Don't tell your mother."

 Less than a minute after his father had left for work, Mark heard the familiar sound of the post coming through the letterbox. It was Wednesday, and sometimes Mark's weekly comic came on a Wednesday, but as he sifted through the letters, there was nothing for him. Mark sighed and then something else was pushed through the letterbox.

My comic, Mark thought, excited.

He decided he would take it to school and read it at dinner time in the classroom while the other kids were freezing outside. He picked up the envelope. It didn't look like the normal one his comic was delivered in. That one was always brown and this one was white. There was something else about this one that struck him as odd – the name M. Russell was written in black pen on the front. He put it with the rest of the mail and went to the kitchen to make something quick for breakfast.

 Mark gobbled down some dry shredded wheat and washed it down with a glass of water. He picked up his school bag and headed for the front door. He was about to open it when he glanced down at the white envelope on the hall table.

Maybe it is my comic, he thought, *maybe they're using different envelopes.*

He picked up the envelope. It seemed to be slightly heavier than normal, and he could feel something at the top.

A free gift, he thought, and his heart quickened.

He loved the free gifts that often came with the comic.

He ripped open the top of the envelope and as he did he felt something prick the palm of his left hand. He dropped the envelope and looked at his hand. The only thing that suggested he'd hurt himself was a tiny indentation in the palm. There wasn't even any blood. Mark picked up the envelope and looked inside. There was no sign of his comic. He threw it on the table in disgust.

The local newspaper landed on the doormat with a quiet thud. Mark looked at the clock on the wall in the hallway. He had ten minutes to get to school. He'd already forgotten about his hand. He picked up the newspaper, threw it on top of the white envelope and left the house, remembering to lock the door behind him.

He hadn't seen the photograph on the front page of the newspaper. It was a photograph of a greyish-brown snake.

CHAPTER TWENTY ONE

The first thing Smith noticed when he picked up the local newspaper was the image on the front page. It was a photograph of a snake poised as if about to strike. Smith read the headline at the top and immediately made a mental note never to trust anybody ever again, no matter who vouches for them. 'Black Mamba kills local man.'

He took the newspaper with him to the kitchen and switched on the kettle. While he waited for it to boil, he read the lead article in the paper. As he read, he was reminded of a conversation he'd had the day before. There on the front page of a newspaper that the majority of the people of York read was his chat with the owner of the Lofthouse's franchise, Tommy Bonner. It was quoted almost word for word. The only thing missing was the metal contraption in the envelope.

Whitton came in with Laura in her arms. "I had the weirdest dream. I dreamt that I could fly. It was really quite surreal. What's up with you?" She'd noticed the frown on Smith's face.

"That bloke we spoke to yesterday," Smith said. "Chalmers' friend went to the papers with what I told him yesterday about how Frank Broadbent was killed. The shit is going to hit the fan with this one."

Whitton placed Laura in her chair and picked up the paper.

"Are you sure it was the DCI's friend?" she asked when she'd got the general gist of the article.

"Who else? Apart from our team, Tommy Bonner is the only person who knew about this."

"It might not be as bad as you think," Whitton said although she knew something like this in the local paper could only be bad news.

"I'm going to be in deep shit for this. I thought I could trust the man. I only told him what we knew because he's ex-job and I thought it might jog his memory about something to do with Frank Broadbent."

"What time are you going in?"

"Ten. Brownhill seems to think we'll be better equipped to come up with something new if we're all well rested. Do you want me to drop Laura off at daycare on my way?"

"We can all go in together. It's still only nine. Do you mind feeding her while I jump in the shower? And don't worry too much – you know what the press is like, there will be some other story tomorrow and this snake thing will be forgotten about."

* * *

When Smith and Whitton went inside the station, Smith knew straight away from the expression on Brownhill's face that the DI had read the local paper.

"Smith," she said. "My office now."

Smith looked at Whitton who offered a sympathetic smile. He followed Brownhill down the corridor towards her office. He almost had to run to keep up.

"I assume this is your doing," Brownhill threw the morning paper on the desk in front of Smith.

"I suppose it is," Smith knew he couldn't deny it. "I thought we could trust the bloke. He's ex-job, and Chalmers vouched for him."

"Do you realise what you've done?"

"At least they didn't print the bit about how the snake venom was injected." The article had merely stated that Frank Broadbent had died due to the effects of the poison from a Black Mamba. How the venom ended up in his system wasn't mentioned.

"And maybe it wasn't even the owner of the restaurant who blabbed," Smith added.

"'A colleague of Mr Broadbent's at Lofthouse's family restaurant spoke of how much he will be missed'" Brownhill read out loud. "Of course it was the owner of the restaurant. Who else knows about this?"

"What's the plan, boss?"

"Damage control. The press will want more, and we're going to give them more. No, *you're* going to give them more."

"Boss?"

"I'm going to arrange a press conference," Brownhill told him. "And you are going to head up that conference."

"Do you think that's a good idea?"

"Do you think we've got a choice?"

"I suppose not," Smith sighed. "When's it going to happen?"

"I'll let you know. Get hold of Neil, the press liaison officer. He'll tell you what you can and cannot say. Damage control, remember?"

Chalmers was in his office staring at his computer screen. Smith went straight in.

"I thought you said Tommy Bonner was a man I could trust," Smith came straight to the point.

"Good morning to you too," Chalmers looked up. "What the hell are you talking about?"

"He leaked what I told him yesterday to the press."

"Tommy wouldn't do that. I've known Tommy Bonner for thirty-odd years and I can tell you it wasn't him."

"Who else could it be? He was the only one who knows about the Black Mamba."

"It wasn't Tommy. I'll bet my life on it. Anyway, why would he do that? What would he gain from it?"

"The name of his restaurant was in the paper," Smith said. "Free advertising."

"I've never heard anything so ridiculous." Chalmers took out his mobile phone and dialled a number. "Ask him yourself."

Smith took the phone from him.

"Lofthouse's," Tommy Bonner answered. "How can I help you?"

"Tommy," Smith said. "This is DS Smith. We spoke yesterday."

"Is this about this morning's paper?" Tommy said before Smith had a chance to say anything. "I was about to get hold of you. I'm so sorry about that."

"So, it was you then?'

"What? Of course, it wasn't me. I know who the leak is and trust me she's had a severe bollocking. She won't be in a hurry to do that again."

"Who was it?"

"A young woman who works for me, Janet. She told me everything. She was listening in at the door when we spoke yesterday."

The sound of footsteps by the door, Smith thought.

It all made sense now.

"Told you," Chalmers said when Smith gave him back the phone.

"Tommy Bonner is old school – he hates the press, and there's no way he'd hand them a present like this on a plate."

"Sorry, boss," Smith said. "I should never have doubted you."

"Make sure it doesn't happen again."

"Brownhill is talking about a press conference. She wants me to speak to the liaison officer first."

"Probably for the best. You do have a bit of a loose tongue sometimes."

Smith was about to try and defend himself when his mobile phone started to ring in his pocket.

"Smith," he answered it.

"I want to live," said the man on the other end of the line.

CHAPTER TWENTY TWO

Morgan Russell was busy with an urgent order when his mobile phone rang. He looked at the screen and sighed. It was the number for the office of the school his son, Mark attended. The first thought that came into his head was that Mark was in trouble. Why else would the school phone him?

"Hello," he answered tentatively.

"Mr Russell, this is Theresa Hawkins. I'm the secretary here at your son's school. It's about Mark."

What's he done? Morgan thought.

"I think you'd better come and collect him. He's been sick and it looks like he's coming down with a fever. He needs to see a doctor."

Morgan Russell arrived at the school fifteen minutes later. His boss had been less than pleased. When he saw his son slumped in the office, he hardly recognised him. Mark's face was deathly pale, his eyelids drooped, and he had beads of sweat on his forehead. His left hand was bandaged.

"Dad," Mark croaked.

"What happened?" Morgan asked.

"I don't feel well."

"I think you'd better take him to a doctor." It was Theresa Hawkins, the secretary who'd phone earlier.

"Come on, my boy," Morgan helped him off the chair. "Let's get you out of here."

"I don't want to go to the doctors," Mark pleaded from the back seat of the car. "I just want to sleep."

Mark didn't like doctors. He'd had a bad experience when he was five years old. A junior doctor had given him an injection, but he'd hit a nerve. Mark still remembered the pain like it was yesterday.

"OK, my boy," Morgan said. "I'll take you home, but if you don't feel any better later, you're going straight to the doctor."

Morgan helped his son inside the house, laid him on the lounge suite and covered him in a blanket.

"Is there anything you need?" he asked.

"My hand's sore," Mark told him. "It really hurts."

"What happened to your hand?"

"The envelope," Mark said faintly. "I thought it was my comic."

"What envelope?"

Mark didn't reply. His eyes rolled back and only the whites were visible.

"Mark," Morgan grabbed hold of his hand. "Mark."

It was clear his son could no longer hear him. His eyelids were now swollen, and he was breathing erratically. Morgan carefully unwrapped the bandage and gasped. His son's whole hand was swollen. There was a small blister on the palm surrounded by skin that had turned blue.

Morgan took out his phone and dialled 999. He informed the operator he needed an ambulance urgently and gave the man the address. He ended the call and looked at his son. His mouth was open and Morgan could see that his tongue was swollen.

Morgan waited by the front door for the ambulance to arrive. He glanced down at the white envelope on the table in the hallway. It had been opened and there was something protruding from the top. Morgan picked it up and opened the envelope wider. Inside was a small metal object. Underneath the metal contraption there was a piece of paper. Morgan took it out and read what was written on it.

CHAPTER TWENTY THREE

"Who is this?" Smith said.

"My name is Morgan Russell," the man said. "Your number was on a piece of paper in an envelope that was delivered to my house. It's my son – he's really ill."

Smith felt sick. "Did he... Did he open the envelope?"

"I think so. He said something about an envelope. His hand is all swollen."

Smith had to think hard. "Phone an ambulance right now."

"I called 999. There's one on the way. I don't know what's wrong with my boy. The school phoned. He didn't want to go to the doctor. He's terrified of doctors. Why is it taking them so long?"

"OK," Smith said. "Try to stay calm. They will be there soon. What does it say on the piece of paper?"

"Something about a special prize. It doesn't really make any sense."

"Does it mention a gift?"

The line was quiet for a few seconds.

"Yes," Morgan said. "It says a gift from a Bitis Gabonica. Hold on – I think the ambulance is outside."

"I'm going to arrange someone to help you. We'll come to the hospital as soon as we can. Keep your phone on you."

Smith ended the call and brought up Kenny Bean's number. The eccentric pathologist answered immediately.

"Detective, what can I interest you in today?"

"Kenny. I need Dr Marx."

"Join the queue."

"This is urgent," Smith said. "Where is she?"

"Standing right beside me. We were just getting ready to open up a corpse which has definitely seen better days. Hold on."

"Hello," Dr Marx said.

"This is DS Smith. I need your help. I believe there's been another snake venom victim."

"I see," she said calmly.

"What does Bitis Gabonica mean?"

"The Gaboon Viper. Longest fangs in the snake world."

"What happens when it bites you?"

"It depends on the venom yield of course, but initially there will be localized swelling, blistering and pain. Convulsions and internal bleeding could occur, but it all depends on the person bitten."

"It was a ten-year-old boy."

"He needs urgent medical attention."

"He's getting it," Smith said. "His name is Mark Russell and he's being brought in as we speak. Could you intercept him when he gets there? They're going to need your expertise. I'll be there as soon as I can."

"There's been another one," Smith told Chalmers when he got off the phone. "Young lad. Looks like the same thing as Frank Broadbent. My number was on the bottom of the note in the envelope."

"Who's doing this, Smith?" the DI asked.

"I really have no idea. I'm going to the hospital."

* * *

Smith found Dr Marx by the reception desk at York City Hospital. She was talking to a middle-aged man in a white coat.

"I got here as soon as I could," Smith told her. "How's Mark Russell doing?"

"It doesn't look good," the man told him. "Doctor Henry Thule. Dr Marx has briefed me on the level of toxicity of this particular venom and it appears young Mark has received a rather large dose. The necrosis is already extensive. He'll be lucky not to lose his hand if he survives."

"If he survives?" Smith said. "Don't you keep anti-venom?"

"I'm afraid not. We really have no call for it."

Smith couldn't believe what he was hearing. "Surely you can get hold of some?"

"Detective," Dr Marx said. "Even if we did organise the anti-venom, it would take too long, and the poison already in his system has done the damage. All we can try to do now is to manage the symptoms."

"Which are?"

"Like I said, it depends on the boy's constitution, but it's likely his blood has already become incoagulable and there's internal bleeding. They are doing everything they can for him."

"Where's his father?" Smith asked.

"He was in the canteen the last time I spoke to him," Dr Thule said.

Morgan Russell was sitting with his head in his hands in the canteen. He was the only person there.

"Mr Russell?" Smith approached him.

"That's right. Is there any news about my boy?"

"My name is Detective Sergeant Smith. We spoke on the phone earlier."

"They said it's snake poison," Morgan said. "How is that possible?"

Smith didn't know what to tell him.

"We don't know yet," was all he could think of. "Is Mrs Russell on her way?"

"It's Mrs Dunn now. We're divorced. I left a message at her work. She's not answering her mobile. Do you know if Mark is going to be alright?"

"They are doing everything they can," Smith reassured him. "He's in good hands."

Mark Russell died two hours later. The quantity of venom that attacked his system was just too much for his young body to fight. The fast-acting poison had caused his blood pressure to drop so suddenly, his heart just couldn't cope and stopped beating. The doctors did everything they could but in the end, they just couldn't revive him.

CHAPTER TWENTY FOUR

The atmosphere in the small conference room was dire. Smith, Whitton, Brownhill, Yang Chu and Bridge sat in silence. They all appeared preoccupied with their own personal thoughts. Every one of them had experienced more death than most, but whenever there was a child involved the experience was always much more unbearable. Brownhill took a deep breath and glanced at the despondent-looking detectives sitting around the table.

"What happened to Mark Russell was a tragedy," she began. "And that is all the more reason to find who is responsible. Smith."

Smith cleared his throat. "Mark Russell opened an envelope that was addressed to M Russell. He father's name is Morgan, so there is no way to tell if the envelope was for him or his son. Mr Russell told me his son subscribes to a weekly comic and assumed that was what the envelope contained."

"Where was the father when the boy opened the envelope?" Bridge asked.

"He was running late for work. Mark said he'd make his own way to school. He'd done it before. He was injected with the venom, and he went to school unaware what the poison was doing to him. I received a phone call from Morgan Russell. It was the same as the first one."

"I want to live." Brownhill reminded them.

The door opened and Chalmers came in with Dr Lillian Marx. Smith watched as Whitton looked her up and down and frowned. He gave his wife his *I told you so* look. Bridge pulled out a chair and Dr Marx sat down next to him. Chalmers remained standing.

"I've asked Dr Marx here this morning to see if we can shed some light on what has happened in the past few days," he said. "Dr Marx."

"Please call me Lillian." She didn't stand up. "I have to be honest and say I haven't seen anything like this before. The two snakes chosen were two with especially virulent venom. Very few people have survived a bite from a Black Mamba without anti-venom being administered immediately, and it's the complications from the poison from a Gaboon Viper that often causes death. Does anybody have any questions?"

"There's something I've been thinking about," Bridge said. "How does the killer know the recipient of the envelope will open it immediately? They could be away or they could just ignore it. Doesn't the snake venom lose its strength outside the snake's body?"

"I'm afraid not," Dr Marx replied. "Snake venom can retain its toxicity for up to ten years after being extracted from the host."

"I have a question," Smith looked her in the eyes. "How the hell does somebody get hold of snake venom?"

Dr Marx returned his gaze. "I believe I've already answered that question. The only place to obtain such poison is on the black market."

"What about snake parks?" Yang Chu said. "Zoos?"

"Impossible."

"Somebody has managed to procure snake venom," Smith had raised his voice. "I was led to believe you were an expert in the field. Think. Where the hell did they get it from?"

Everybody in the room turned to look at him. Even Whitton looked shocked, and she had seen much worse from her husband over the years.

"There is nobody I know of in this country who could possibly get hold of the venom from these snakes," Dr Marx looked furious.

"And from oversees?" Whitton said calmly. "What if they brought it in from abroad?"

"I want you to make me a list of all the people you've come across who have access to these poisons," Smith said.

"I can't possibly be expected to…"

"I think that's enough," Brownhill cut her up. "This isn't getting us anywhere. Let's look at the victims."

"Frank Broadbent and Mark Russell," Yang Chu reminded everyone.

"And we have to add Morgan Russell into the equation," Whitton added. "He could just have easily opened that envelope."

"Right," Brownhill said. "We'll have a closer look at them."

Smith was miles away. He was thinking about something else altogether. "Why was my mobile phone number on the notes inside the envelopes?" he spoke to the wall opposite him. "I don't know what it means. What has this got to do with me?"

"It's certainly personal," Chalmers said. "Whoever this maniac is, he knows you. And if he knows you surely he'd know you'd be involved in the investigation anyway, so why go one step further and ask the victims to phone your number?"

"For the time being we'll concentrate on those victims," Brownhill said. "Something must link them together."

"With respect, boss," Smith looked at the DI. "I don't think they're connected."

"What makes you think that?"

"Because I've never met either of them. Why put my number there when these people have nothing to do with me. What would be the point?"

"I agree with DS Smith." It was Dr Marx. "I'm no detective, but it doesn't take one to see that this is all about Smith."

"So, are you saying the victims were selected at random?" Bridge said.

"I am," Smith answered the question. "And as such I believe we'll be wasting our time looking into the lives of Frank Broadbent and the Russells."

The room went silent for a moment. Everybody seemed to be digesting what Smith had just said.

"Are we one hundred percent certain the boy was injected by the same method as Frank Broadbent?" Yang Chu broke the silence.

"Webber has the envelope and the metal contraption that was inside it," Smith told him. "We'll know for certain later, but it looks like the same thing. Same note with my number at the bottom. It was handwritten like the other one, but the post stamp was from Whitby."

"So, he travels around to post them," Yang Chu said.

"Another dead end then," Bridge sighed.

"Does anybody have any suggestions?" Brownhill asked.

"Find out where that venom came from," Smith wasn't giving up.

"I'll do a bit of digging," Dr Marx offered and smiled at him.

"Thank you. Maybe if we have a list of names, one of them will jump out at me."

CHAPTER TWENTY FIVE

Smith remained behind with Brownhill when the rest of the team had left. The DI needed to discuss the imminent press conference in light of what had happened to Mark Russell that morning.

"This is going to get out whether we like it or not," she said. "What with social media and the like, so we're going to have to bring it up. But we have to be very careful not to cause any unnecessary panic. You know how things can blow up."

"Do we mention the way the killer operates?"

"Definitely not. Not yet."

"Then what exactly do I say to them? How do I explain how these two people ended up with deadly snake venom in them?"

Brownhill clearly didn't have an answer for him.

"Well?" Smith urged.

Brownhill looked at her watch. "We have a few hours to come up with something. Have you spoken to the press liaison officer yet?"

"I haven't had time, what with the death of the young boy."

"Neil is expecting you. He's good and he'll come up with something you can tell them."

"Do you think this is going to happen again, boss?" Smith asked.

"I don't know," Brownhill replied and from the tone of her voice it was clear she'd been thinking the same thing. "I really don't know."

* * *

Smith found Neil Walker in his office at the end of the corridor. The press liaison officer spent most of his time cooped up there with his eyes glued to his laptop.

"Take a seat," he beckoned to the chair opposite him.

Smith sat down. "I don't know how much you know about the investigation."

"I have been given copies of all the relevant files," Neil told him.

"How do you want to play this? Two people have been injected with snake venom in the space of a few days. They were both victims of a really elaborate letter bomb."

"Do you want to tell the press that?"

"Are you being serious? We've got enough on our plates without having every Tom, Dick and Harry ringing in to tell us about every suspicious-looking envelope that lands on their doorsteps."

"You realise that it's going to get out eventually don't you?"

"Probably, but I'd rather we were left in peace to do our jobs without having to deal with time-wasters."

"I've come up with a spin," Neil said.

"A spin?"

"If we inform the press that two people were killed this week with snake venom, they are going to ask more pressing questions, and if we don't have a reasonable explanation, they are going to do what they do best."

"Speculate," Smith said.

"Exactly. And you know from past experiences that speculation is often worse than the truth."

Smith knew that very well. They were words used very often by his bungling Superintendent. "So, what do you suggest I tell them? What's this about a spin?"

"You will tell them about the envelopes and the metal contraptions inside. And you will tell them exactly how these people were injected."

Smith was confused. "I thought you implied we weren't to do that. It'll only cause panic."

"It'll keep them happy for a while - It's quite a sensational story don't you think? What you are also going to hint at is you are looking into a possible link between the two victims. You don't mention their names of course."

"Out of sympathy for their families?"

"You catch on quickly, DS Smith. If the public believe these people were targeted for some particular reason, they won't panic. What do you think?"

"I think I'm the wrong man to head up the press conference. You do know about my phone number on the notes inside the envelopes?"

"Naturally, but no good will come out of making that information public just yet. The fact that an unusual murder weapon was used will probably be more than enough for the press for now. But you can juice it up if you like. You've brought in an expert – you have a number of ongoing lines of enquiry."

"We're still waiting for the final forensics reports to come in?" Smith added.

Neil Walker smiled. "See, you are definitely the right man for the job. The press conference is scheduled for six this evening. In the meantime, I'll prepare a press release, and we'll take it from there. Keep me informed of any new developments. Don't worry – you'll be just fine."

Smith's head was pounding as he closed Neil Walker's door behind him and headed for the canteen. He needed the strongest coffee the machine could offer him. Whitton, Bridge and Yang Chu had obviously had the same idea. They were sitting in silence next to the window. Smith got two double espressos from the machine and sat next to Whitton.

"Are you planning on staying awake for a few days?" she nodded to the contents of his coffee cup.

Smith took a long drink. "I've got a press conference at six. I've just had a meeting with the liaison officer. He came up with an idea – a spin he called it."

He told them about his conversation with Neil Walker.

"Do you think it'll work?" Bridge asked. "Do you think they'll fall for it?"

"There's nothing to fall for. I'm telling them the truth."

"Apart from the link between the two victims," Yang Chu pointed out.

"Brownhill asked us to look into the victims," Smith said. "So I won't exactly be lying."

"Rather you than me," Bridge said. "I hate press conferences. They always seem to ask you stuff you're not ready for."

"It can't be helped. Unfortunately, with all the social media platforms these days we need to get in first."

"Speculation is much more damaging to our reputation than the truth," Whitton quoted Superintendent Smyth word for word.

Smith smiled at her. His headache was easing off and he felt much more relaxed than he had done earlier.

"Do you reckon this snake guy is going to strike again?" Yang Chu asked.

"I have no idea," Smith replied. "Maybe he'll stop when he sees his work all over the newspapers."

CHAPTER TWENTY SIX

Lisa Sweeney nudged her front door open and went inside. She stepped to the side of the pile of mail on the mat by the door and took the bulging shopping bags through to the kitchen. She piled them on the table, opened the fridge and took out a bottle of white wine. She got a glass from the rack on the sink, unscrewed the wine and poured it into the glass full to the brim. Lisa gulped down half the glass and turned her attention to the shopping on the table. She packed it away and filled up her wine glass once more. It had been a long day. The department store where she worked as cosmetics manager had begun its three-week long sale, and Lisa had been forced to work twice as hard as usual. She would be glad when the Christmas season was over.

Lisa turned her attention to the pile of letters by her front door. Rejection letters, probably.

Lisa aspired to become a writer – she'd written short stories and poems when she was younger, and she'd taken it up again years later. She hated her job, and hoped that one day an agent or publisher would *discover* her, and she would be able to write all day, every day.

Lisa was running out of agents and publishers to send her material to. Not only had she chosen a niche genre to write in – she was something of a traditionalist and only contacted those who still accepted manuscripts on paper. She picked up the pile of correspondence and took it through to the kitchen. Before sifting through it, she poured herself another glass of wine. She had a feeling she would need it, one way or another. Experience had taught her that the thicker the envelope, the more likely it was to bring bad news.

A returned manuscript with a covering letter to inform her that she wasn't quite the right *fit* for that particular publisher or agency.

Lisa opened the heavier envelopes first – it was always better to get the bad news out of the way first. It was as she'd expected – her painstaking work had been returned to her. All of the manuscripts were in the same condition as they were when she sent them. They obviously hadn't even been read.

The wine was taking effect now. Lisa knew that Wayne wouldn't be too impressed when he came home. He hated it when she drank by herself, but Lisa no longer really cared. She was tiring of him anyway. When she first met him he'd encouraged her in her dreams, but recently he suggested she give it all up and face the reality that short romantic stories and love poems were never going to make her rich. Lisa poured another glass and picked up the last envelope in the pile. It was much lighter than the rest and her name and address had been written in black block capitals on the front. She didn't know if it was the effect of drinking the white wine too quickly or something else, but she could feel her face beginning to flush.

This could be the one, she thought. *This could be that moment that only happens once in a lifetime.*

She looked at the writing on the front – The letters slanted slightly to the right, but it was incredibly neat. There was no return address on the back of the envelope to suggest where it had come from, and the postal stamp told her it had been posted in Leeds. Lisa tried to recall if she'd even sent a manuscript to anybody in Leeds, but she'd sent out so many in the past few years she'd lost count of who they'd been sent to.

"Here goes," she said and finished the wine in her glass.

With one swift movement she ripped open the top of the envelope, something cut into her wrist and she dropped it onto the table.

Paper cut, she thought.

She carefully picked up the envelope again, turned it upside down and shook it. A single piece of paper fell out and landed next to her wine glass. Lisa picked it up and opened it.

This could be the moment that only happens once in a lifetime, she thought again.

Then she read what was written on the sheet of paper:

'CONGRATULATIONS. YOU HAVE BEEN CHOSEN TO RECEIVE A SPECIAL PRIZE – A GIFT FROM A DABOIA RUSSELII. YOUR REWARD IS OBLIVION. SHOULD YOU DECIDE NOT TO ACCEPT THIS PRIZE, PHONE THE NUMBER BELOW AND REPEAT THESE FOUR SIMPLE WORDS – I WANT TO LIVE.'

There was a mobile phone number at the bottom of the page.

Lisa was confused and the effects of almost an entire bottle of wine didn't help. She put down the piece of paper, poured what was left in the bottle of wine into her glass and read the words again. The paper cut on her wrist was stinging now. She looked at it closely and saw that it wasn't a paper cut – it was a small pin-prick sized hole out of which oozed a single drop of blood. The skin was inflamed around the hole, and she was certain it was swelling before her eyes.

She raised the glass to her lips but her fingers suddenly weakened and she couldn't get a grip on it. It dropped to the kitchen floor and smashed onto the tiles.

Lisa sat back in her chair. She could taste blood inside her mouth – a metallic tang she'd last tasted once before when she'd walked into a door in a drunken state and knocked two of her teeth out. She felt incredibly weak, her limbs felt heavy and she was now finding it difficult to breathe. The inflammation on her wrist had spread halfway up her arm. She breathed in, but couldn't get enough air into her lungs. A dizziness crept over her, she closed her eyes and drifted off.

Lisa Sweeney had been right about one thing:

This was definitely a moment that happens only once in a lifetime.

CHAPTER TWENTY SEVEN

The press conference wasn't due to start for another hour but the car park outside the station was already full when Smith went outside for a smoke. He slipped out of sight around the corner of the building, lit a cigarette and went over in his head what he was and wasn't going to tell the journalists. He was having doubts about whether Neil Walker's plan was going to work. Experience had taught him that the press weren't easy to fool – they had some kind of sixth sense and were expert at spotting lies.

Smith heard footsteps approach and slunk into a doorway.

"Great minds think alike." It was Chalmers.

The DCI lit his own cigarette and shivered. "It's going to drop right below zero tonight they reckon. Are you all set to face the gauntlet?"

"No," Smith said. "You're welcome to take my place if you want."

"Not bloody likely. I've done my fair share of vulture-appeasing over the years. Just go with what Walker told you and you'll be fine. Do you still have no idea who could be doing this?"

"I've thought about pretty much nothing else since this whole nightmare began," Smith said. "And I've come up with nothing. Dr Marx is putting together a list of people she's met over the years who could possibly know someone who could manage to get hold of snake venom."

"What do you make of her?"

"She's a bit odd. She loves snakes, and that in itself is odd, but she seems OK. Bridge likes her."

"Bridge likes anything with a pulse and a pair of X chromosomes," Chalmers laughed and threw his cigarette butt into the distance. "You'd better get in there."

"Let's get it over with, shall we?"

* * *

Smith went inside the main conference room, walked past the men and women already seated as though they were invisible and took a seat next to DI Brownhill at the head of the main table facing the press. The noise inside was unbearable.

"Are you ready?" Brownhill said.

"Of course," Smith lied. "Is the Super attending? He usually doesn't miss these for the world."

"He was somehow persuaded his presence wasn't necessary at this one. You have friends in high places, Smith."

Right on cue, Chalmers walked in and sat next to Smith.

"Thanks, boss," Smith said to him.

"What for?"

"Getting old Smyth out of the way for this thing. How did you do that?"

Chalmers tapped his nose. "Trade secret."

Brownhill sighed and shook her head.

The room had filled up. Those arriving late had to put up with standing room only. Not enough chairs had been provided. Smith spotted Dr Lillian Marx at the back of the room. She was deep in conversation with someone. The man had his back to Smith but still he seemed vaguely familiar. There was something about him that Smith recognised.

"Let's make a start shall we?" Brownhill said.

"I'll lead off," Chalmers offered and tapped his nose again. "In Smyth's absence I mean."

He stood up and scanned the crowd of people in front of him. He switched on the microphone and coughed into it. The crowd turned to look at him and the deafening din ceased.

"Good evening," Chalmers began. "Thank you all for coming. I'll hand you over to the lead detective in this investigation. DS Smith."

Smith turned on his own microphone. "Good evening. You all know what this is about so I'll keep it brief."

Neil Walker had suggested those words.

"I will ask you to keep any questions you have until the end. On Monday of this week an alert was put out after a man failed to turn up for work. He was found dead in his kitchen. We now know the cause of death was poison from a Black Mamba Snake."

There were a few gasps from Smith's captive audience.

"And earlier today," Smith continued. "A young boy became ill at school – his father took him home, but his condition deteriorated, and he died a few hours ago. He too had snake venom in his system. From a Gaboon Viper. We now know beyond a shadow of a doubt how the venom found its way there." He paused for a second. Not for effect, but because he was finding it difficult to breathe and he needed some time to take in air.

"Both victims had envelopes sent to them," Smith had managed to compose himself. "Inside these envelopes were small metal contraptions that contained the snake venom. The venom was administered by a needle that was triggered by whoever opened the envelope. We are looking into a connection between the two victims, and we will work round the clock until whoever is responsible for this is caught."

Another pause. Smith knew what he said next would leave him no room to breathe.

"Any questions?"

A man in the front row raised his hand. "DS Smith you said these people were killed with snake venom?"

"That's correct."

"Where did this venom come from?"

"The first one was from a Black Mamba..."

"We know that," the man butted in. "Do you know how the killer got his hands on the venom?"

"We're still working on that."

"And *how* exactly are you working on it?"

"We've brought in an expert in the field, and she's proving to be very helpful."

"Detective," a woman at the back had raised her hand. "The connection between the two victims – could you elaborate on that?"

"Not at the moment. The identities of the deceased will be released in due course, but I'm sure you can understand what their families must be going through right now. They need to be left in peace for the time being."

A man to Smith's left stood up. "Do you believe the general public has anything to worry about?"

It was a question Smith had been dreading. For the simple fact that he had no answer to it.

"No," he lied. "As I said we are looking into a connection between the victims and we are confident we will bring a swift end to this investigation."

"DS Smith," a voice Smith immediately recognised shouted from the back of the room.

Smith looked straight at him and his breath left him once more. It was the man Dr Lillian Marx had been talking to before the conference. Smith knew him well. His name was Matthew Mclean and he was the brother of one of only two women Smith had ever loved. Lucy McLean had been killed by a maniac out to hurt Smith. Smith was the one who found her with her throat sliced open on the floor of his bathroom.

Smith had last seen Matt Mclean a few months earlier. Matt had been in town and suggested they meet up for a drink. The meeting had started off well, but after more and more to drink, Matt had become aggressive and accused Smith of being to blame for his sister's murder. The night had ended with Matt issuing a veiled threat and leaving. Smith had actually put the incident to the back of his mind. And now he was back.

What is Matt McLean doing at this press conference?

"Go on," Smith urged.

"DS Smith," Matt said again. "Are you sure you're telling us everything?"

"I've answered all your questions," was all Smith could think of to say.

"That's not what I asked. I get the feeling you're leaving something out."

Smith really didn't know what to say. Matt McLean was staring at him without blinking.

"I'll take your silence as a yes then," he said smugly. "There's something you're not telling us."

Smith's mouth refused to work.

Help came from a familiar source.

"Of course we're not telling you everything." Chalmers had stood up and was staring Matt McLean directly in the eye. "Are you so naïve you think we give the press everything we have? Is this your first press conference, lad?"

A few sniggers could be heard from the crowd.

"Let me tell you a few things. Firstly, we are not obliged to give you anything, but we've worked well together in the past and you'll be surprised how often you lot have helped us catch criminals. So we're courteous enough to share certain information with you. Secondly, what do you think would happen if we divulged every scrap of info we have with you? Apart from this conference lasting about a week that is."

More people started to laugh. Smith could feel the relief surge through his whole body. He looked to see how Matt McLean had taken Chalmers' dressing down, but he was gone.

CHAPTER TWENTY EIGHT

Smith needed a drink. He'd left the large conference room as soon as possible and headed outside for a smoke. He finished his first cigarette and lit the end of another one with it. The press conference had really taken it out of him. It had started well but Matt McLean's appearance had really unnerved him.

What was he doing there?

As far as Smith was aware, Matt had nothing to do with the press. He smoked the last drag of his cigarette, kept it in his lungs for as long as he could manage and exhaled a cloud of smoke.

He went back inside the station to look for Chalmers. He was going to suggest a drink at the Hog's Head to thank the DCI for sticking his neck out for him. Brownhill was talking to PC Baldwin by the front desk when he walked past. Smith was halfway down the corridor that led to the offices when he heard Brownhill call his name. He turned around and walked back to the front desk.

"What's up, boss?"

"A young woman has been found dead at home on Grey Street. Her boyfriend found her slumped on a chair in the kitchen and called it in. Uniform was dispatched and it's confirmed that she is dead. Bridge and Yang Chu are there now. I want you to get down there too."

"Can't someone else deal with it?" Smith said. "I'm knackered after the press conference and this shitty day."

"I appreciate that, but I think you'll want to go. It looks like we've got another one."

"Another one?"

"Bridge called a short while ago. They found another envelope with the name handwritten on the front. And there was another note with your number on it."

"Shit," Smith said and closed his eyes. "I don't know how much more of this I can take. What's the address again?"

Smith drove far too quickly to the address he'd been given for the woman who'd been found dead in the kitchen. He felt quite sick – if what Brownhill had told him was correct three people had died from snake venom in the space of a few days. All three of them were told to contact him on his mobile number and say the words, 'I want to live.' He still didn't have the faintest idea what it all meant. The press conference had left his head spinning, and seeing Matt McLean there had made it worse.

What was Lucy McLean's brother doing at a press conference? Smith thought, *and why the sudden disappearing act?*

Those thoughts were pushed aside when Smith parked outside the address Brownhill had given him. Yang Chu's Ford Focus was there as was Grant Webber's car. An ambulance was parked directly outside the house. Smith experienced a flashing sensation of déjà vu. How many times had he arrived at this exact crime scene? Even the crowd of people gathered seemed the same – like extras in a movie he had been forced to watch over and over again.

Smith walked past a middle-aged PC, nodded and went inside the house. Grant Webber was in the kitchen going through the motions. The dead woman was still sitting on the chair. Smith moved in to get a closer look. He determined that once upon a time she'd been a pretty twenty-something. Her hair was cut short and hung just below her jaw line. Her blue eyes were open and the skin on her face was now almost the same colour as them – dark blue. Her lips had swollen, as had her eyelids.

"This is a crime scene, Smith," Webber said by way of a greeting.

"We both know that's not true, Webber. This is where she died. The crime scene is still a mystery to us. Where's the note?"

"Bagged and sealed," the head of forensics told him. "It's the same as the others apart from the Latin name of the snake."

"Do we know what snake venom was used this time?"

"I called Dr Marx as soon as I got here. Russell's Viper. Apparently it's the snake responsible for more fatalities than any other worldwide."

"Great," Smith said. "How long has she been dead?"

Webber's grin took Smith by surprise. "You never cease to amaze me, Smith. Do I have to remind you for the thousandth time who the detective is here?"

"It's been a long, shitty day, Webber. Rough guess?"

"No more than an hour or two. But don't quote me on that. Bridge and Yang Chu have spoken to the boyfriend. He's the one who called it in. Why don't you change the habit of a lifetime and just do your job. I'd quite like to do mine in peace and quiet for a while."

"Thanks, Grant," Smith said with a wry smile.

He knew how Webber hated it when Smith used his first name.

Bridge and Yang Chu were in the living room. They were talking to a man who looked to be in his early thirties. He was sitting in a single-seater chair, his face was very pale and his eyes were bloodshot. Bridge spotted Smith and walked over.

"What have we got?" Smith asked even though he knew exactly what they were dealing with.

"Lisa Sweeney," Bridge told him. "Twenty eight years old. Her boyfriend found her when he got home from work. Called it in straight away."

"What time was this?"

"Around half-six. He works in Leeds and he commutes every day. Lisa usually finishes work at four and gets in at half past."

"Webber doesn't think she's been dead long. We'll know more when we get the prelim path report, but I reckon she got home, opened the envelope and was injected. Her boyfriend probably just missed out on saving her life."

"He's in a bit of a state," Bridge said. "I don't think we're going to get much out of him tonight."

"I don't think there's much to get out of him anyway is there?"

Smith walked up to Lisa Sweeney's boyfriend. He glanced at the clock on the mantelpiece – it was seven-forty-five.

"Sarge," Yang Chu said. "This is Wayne Long. He's Miss Sweeney's boyfriend."

"Wayne," Smith said. "I'm DS Smith. I understand this is hard for you, but I believe you were the one who found Lisa?"

"I can't believe this is happening," Wayne said. "I got home at the same time as normal. I've just found out I got the promotion at work, and I was going to take Lisa out to celebrate."

"What time was this?"

"Six-thirty. I went through to the kitchen and I saw that she'd started celebrating without me."

"What do you mean?"

"There was an empty wine bottle on the table, and a smashed glass on the floor. Lisa sometimes gets a bit carried away when she drinks. That's why when I saw her slumped in the chair I just thought she was drunk."

His top lip started to tremble and Smith was afraid he was about to break down and cry.

"I..." he managed to control himself. "I had a closer look and that's when I realised there was something wrong. Her eyes were open, and her face was a funny colour. What happened to her?"

He gazed up at Smith with pleading eyes.

"We're not sure yet," Smith was really getting tired of lying to people. "I just have one more question and we'll get going. What time do you and Lisa leave for work in the morning?"

"What's that got to do with anything?"

"Please just answer the question, Mr Long."

"I leave before Lisa. At six. And she starts work at eight, so she leaves the house at half-seven."

"Before the morning post is delivered then?"

"Yes."

"Thank you," Smith said. "Is there somebody you can stay with tonight?"

"My brother lives just around the corner. I can stay with him."

"Good," Smith said.

He left the room, walked out of the front door and headed straight for his car.

CHAPTER TWENTY NINE

Smith drove away from yet another murder scene. Away from the ambulance parked outside an unfamiliar house. Away from a grieving boyfriend he'd never met before. He drove without any idea where he was going. He turned onto the road that stretched alongside the Hog's Head, but as he was about to turn left into the car park, he changed his mind. What he needed now wasn't the solace of the bottom of a glass – what he needed now was the solace of two beautiful ladies and two not-so-beautiful dogs.

It was 8:30 when Smith turned the key in the lock and opened his front door. Theakston and Fred jumped up at his legs as he walked into the kitchen. Whitton and Laura were nowhere to be seen. He switched on the kettle and went through to the living room while he waited for it to boil. Whitton was watching something on the TV. She didn't even acknowledge Smith when he came in the room.

He sat next to her on the sofa. "I'm making some coffee. Do you want anything?"

"Where have you been?" Whitton asked without taking her eyes off the television screen.

"Rough day at work. What's wrong?"

"I tried calling you about fifty times. Laura's sick."

"I didn't receive any calls," Smith took out his phone. "Shit. I turned it on silent before the press conference and I forgot to turn it back on. I'm sorry. What's wrong with Laura?"

"Some bug that's going round at daycare. I'm going to keep her off for a few days. My Mum and Dad have offered to have her. I've given her some medicine and she's fast asleep."

"I'm sorry," Smith said again. "It's been a day from hell. I don't know how much more of this I can cope with."

On hearing this Whitton turned to face her husband. She'd never heard him talk like this before.

"What happened?"

"Another woman was killed with snake venom," Smith told her. "A young woman in her twenties. Her boyfriend found her. The switchboard got the call during the press conference."

"How did that go?"

"It started off great, and then Matt McLean appeared and tried to sabotage the whole thing."

"Matt McLean? Lucy's brother?"

"I don't even know what he was doing there. He's not a journo as far as I'm aware. Anyway, I think I can safely say this has probably been one day of my life I wish I could forget all about."

Whitton shuffled closer and wrapped her arms around her husband. "I reckon that kettle ought to have boiled by now. Tea would be nice."

Smith smiled, kissed her on the forehead and went to make the drinks.

Smith put the tea and coffee on the table next to them and sat down again.

"This whole thing is really messing with my head," he said, and took a drink of coffee.

"You need to learn to relax and not take every investigation as a personal attack on you."

"This is personal, Erica. This one is very personal. Whoever is doing this is leaving my mobile number. It couldn't get any more personal."

"Tell me about the press conference," Whitton said.

"Like I said, it started off quite well." Smith ignored her obvious attempt at trying to change the topic of conversation. "Smyth wasn't there so it boded well."

"The Super missed a press conference?"

"Chalmers had a hand in it. Neil Walker prepped me beforehand and told me what I should and shouldn't say. You know what it's like. Keep it vague – give them enough, but just enough. All the questions I was asked were answered and they seemed content with what I'd given them. And then Matt McLean showed up and things got a bit weird."

"What do you mean?"

"It was like he knew everything. I can't put my finger on why, but I got the feeling he knows about the notes with my number on them."

"How can he possibly know that?"

"It's just the way he spoke. He said, 'I get the feeling you're leaving something out.'"

"I think he was just trying to rile you," Whitton said. "He doesn't like you very much. He probably just thought it would be a good opportunity to get back at you. It's quite pathetic if you ask me, and I wouldn't even worry about it."

"I suppose you're right. This whole investigation is playing with my head. I hate it when we have absolutely nothing to go on, and that's pretty much what we have right now. Nothing."

"My Mum and Dad were talking about Christmas," Whitton said. "I know you've never really bothered about Christmas before, but with Laura now I think we should do something nice."

The reason Smith had never really bothered with Christmas before was simple.

It was Christmas Day 1997. Smith was fifteen years old. He'd woken early and the house was in silence. He went outside to the back garden and sat in the early morning sun for a while before venturing further into the garden. Something was different that morning – something Smith couldn't pinpoint. The air felt different. Smith approached the tall trees right at the back of the garden and that's when he found his father swinging from one of the lower branches. He had hanged himself with a thick rope.

That was more than twenty years ago.

"You're right," he said. "I'll go along with anything you've got planned."

"I thought we could have it here," Whitton suggested. "Just us and my parents. We'll cook a nice Christmas Dinner."

"I said I'll go along with anything. I just hope this shitty business is all over by then."

CHAPTER THIRTY

As Smith drove slowly on the icy roads towards the station he had the uneasy feeling he was being observed. The roads were busy with people on their way to work and children on the way to school, but still Smith sensed he was being followed. He glanced in his rear-view mirror for the fifth time in a minute and there it was – a black hatchback. There were two cars in between him and the black hatchback, so Smith couldn't make out the features of the driver behind the tinted windscreen. He stopped at the traffic lights where he usually turned left onto the road that led to the station, but when the lights changed to green Smith carried on straight. He had been driving these streets for years, and knew them like the back of his hand. The black car was still behind him, two cars back. The heavy traffic made it impossible for Smith to increase his speed so he kept it at a steady thirty miles per hour, checking his mirror the whole time.

At the next lights, he turned left onto what he knew was a much quieter road. This road followed the river for a few hundred metres then veered off away from the city centre. There were fewer cars here so Smith pressed his foot harder on the accelerator and the speedometer informed him he was driving at fifty miles per hour, ten over the speed limit for this road. Smith didn't care.

The black hatchback was still there, albeit further behind than it had been before. Smith spotted some cars up ahead on the opposite side of the road. They were driving slowly, so Smith managed to turn right onto a side street in front of them. The black hatchback had to wait for them to pass before it could do the same. Smith came to a halt on the side street a couple of hundred metres further up the road, stopped the engine and got out of the car. The wind was whistling through the narrow road. He watched as the black hatchback turned into the same road and approached. He made himself clearly visible in front of his red Ford Sierra. The other car slowed down and stopped about fifty metres away. As the windows were tinted Smith couldn't see who the driver was. He started to walk up to the car. He was about halfway when he heard a crunch as reverse gear was engaged and the car screeched backwards out of the side road.

Smith ran as fast as he could back to his car, got in and turned the key in the ignition. He drove as fast as he could to the end of the road and then stopped. He looked both left and right but the black hatchback was nowhere to be seen. He slammed both fists on the dashboard and sat for a while with his head in his hands.

What the hell is happening?

Brownhill had scheduled the morning meeting for nine, and when Smith walked in at ten past, the DI was clearly not impressed.

"You're late. And what happened to you last night? You just disappeared without a word to anyone. That is not what I expect from the detective leading the investigation."

Smith's heart was still pounding from the incident with the black hatchback earlier. "Then put someone else in charge. I really couldn't give a toss right now."

Brownhill was clearly about to say something – her mouth opened, but it closed quickly and she opened up a file in front of her instead.

"Lisa Sweeney," she said after a few seconds. "Twenty eight years old. She worked as a manager in one of the large department stores in the town centre. She was found by her boyfriend, Wayne Long at six-thirty yesterday evening. Mr Long initially assumed she was drunk – there was an empty white wine bottle on the table next to her, but when he looked closer he realised she was dead. He called 999 straight away."

"What do we know about her?" Yang Chu asked.

"What the DI just told you, Yang Chu," Smith said. "And that's all we need to know about her. Who she was or what she was isn't relevant here. We have three random victims. They weren't chosen for any particular reason other than they all have letterboxes. Where's the doc?"

"Dr Marx?" Brownhill said. "Busy at the hospital – she'll be in later, and it's good to have you with us again."

Smith gave her a smile by way of an apology for his earlier behaviour.

"I might have come up with a theory," he said and everybody in the room turned to look at him.

"This might seem a bit far-fetched," he began. "But hear me out. Three people have died this week as a result of being injected with snake venom. I am ninety-nine percent sure they were unrelated, and they were just unfortunate victims in all of this. This is all linked to me. Or to be more precise, it's linked to someone who hates me. Someone who wants me to suffer, and if I'm being totally honest here, they're doing a pretty good job so far."

"Do you have any idea who it could be?" Brownhill asked.

"So you don't disagree with me, then?"

"The fact that your mobile number was written at the bottom of the letters the victims received would suggest you have a fair point."

"Yesterday at the press conference, there was a man there who had no business there," Smith continued. "His name is Matt McLean, and as far as I'm aware he has nothing to do with the press."

"The one who asked the awkward questions at the end?" Brownhill said.

"He is the brother of the woman who was killed by Jimmy Fulton. He blames me entirely for her death. He told me as much a few months ago."

"An inkling of a motive then?" Bridge said.

"I've come across stranger motives," Brownhill agreed.

"There's more. The last time I saw Matt Mclean he warned me that it wasn't over. It was a veiled threat if I've ever heard one. And before the press conference began, I saw him talking to our snake doctor and they appeared to know each other quite well."

"What are you implying?" Bridge was suddenly on the defensive. "That Dr Marx has something to do with this?"

"I'm not implying anything. I know what I saw and surely I'm not the only one who thinks it's odd that somebody who has threatened me is seen deep in conversation with somebody we've recently recruited to help us."

"There's no such thing as coincidence?" Yang Chu quoted one of Smith's mantras.

"There isn't. And this morning somebody followed me on the way to work. It was a black hatchback. I know they were following me because I took a very roundabout route and they stayed behind me the whole time. When I stopped in a back street whoever it was caught up, but when they realised they'd been busted they made a hasty getaway."

"Did you see who it was?" This was clearly news to Whitton.

"The windows were tinted," Smith said. "But, as Yang Chu so eloquently put it, there is no such thing as coincidence. Somebody is trying to rattle me."

CHAPTER THIRTY ONE

The man with the lisp put down the morning paper and shivered. It was a shiver of pure delight. He was on the front page for the second time in as many days.

"We're famous," he shouted down the hallway.

He knew his *lovelies* wouldn't understand but he felt compelled to tell them anyway.

He read the newspaper article again. The boy was unfortunate – he had to admit that to himself, but he was also necessary.

Jason Smith must be going out of his mind by now.

The man with the lisp picked up his mobile phone and opened up his search engine. He found the number he was looking for straight away. There was something the press didn't know, and it was something the general public had a right to be aware of. He saved the telephone number and left the house. He walked towards the small shopping complex a couple of hundred of metres from his house. The icy wind was rushing through the streets and there were very few people around. He went inside the phone booth and closed the door behind him.

"York Gazette," the bored-sounding woman answered immediately.

"Good morning," the man with the lisp said. "I would like to communicate regarding the article in your paper."

He had become so used to forming sentences omitting words that would give away his speech impediment it was now second nature.

"Which article would that be, sir?" the monotonous voice enquired.

"The venom article."

"And how can I help you with that?"

"Certain important information was not reported. I have that information. Could I maybe talk to a member of the editorial team?"

"Putting you through."

The man with the lisp held on for a few seconds. He could feel his body temperature rising – he was getting closer and closer to his goal, and it made him feel like he'd never felt before.

"Davies," a man's voice was heard.

"Good morning," the man with the lisp said. "I have information regarding the venom article."

"That was mine," the man called Davies said. "What information are you talking about? You do realise we do not pay for information."

"Your printing it will be payment enough. I have two important things to tell you."

He cursed inwards when he realised he'd just given away his lisp.

"Go ahead," Davies didn't sound too impressed.

He sounded like a man who was used to having his time wasted.

"At the conference, the detective in charge left bits out."

"DS Smith?"

"Affirmative. He omitted to mention his involvement in the deaths."

"What are you trying to say here?" Davies suddenly sounded interested.

"Ask him about the correspondence found at each crime location. Correspondence with the detective's phone number on it. He won't deny it."

"What was the other thing?"

"Pardon me?"

"You said you had two things to tell me."

"There will be another one tomorrow. A particularly quick one. Then there will be one more, and then it will stop. You can print that."

"Could I please have your name?" Davies asked.

"If I had any friends," the man with the lisp said. "They would call me BB."

He ended the call.

He closed the door of the public telephone booth and walked home again. He opened up his car and turned the key in the ignition. There was somewhere he needed to go, and more urgently, there was somebody he needed to meet.

CHAPTER THIRTY TWO

"What do you suggest we do?" Brownhill asked Smith.

The team were still seated in the small conference room for the morning briefing.

"We need to find out more about Dr Lillian Marx," Smith replied. "All we know about the woman is she's recently joined Kenny Bean's team at the hospital and she's an expert on snakes. I want to speak to Dr Bean myself. And I want to find out more about Matt McLean – how long he's been in York, what he's been up to since he's been here. We didn't get much from the envelopes sent by the killer but we did find something we can use."

He looked around the room expectantly.

"The post marks," Whitton exclaimed after a few moments silence.

"Of course," Brownhill was now on the same page. "Those post marks are like a primitive global positioning system. Where were the envelopes posted from?"

She addressed the question to Yang Chu.

"The first one was sent from Richmond, Ma'am," he told her. "The second from Whitby and the latest one was posted in Leeds."

"Which means," Smith said. "If we can put Matt McLean in those three places in the past week, we've got enough to bring him in. I want him found. Whitton, you and Yang Chu look into it. I want to know where he is before the end of the day. I'll be at the hospital if anybody's looking for me."

Smith was almost out of the door when he felt a hand on his shoulder.

"Are you alright?" It was Whitton.

"I'm pissed off," Smith replied.

"Good. Pissed off is good. Stay pissed off – it's how you've managed to crack most of your cases. We'll catch this maniac. And we've got a lovely Christmas to look forward to."

Smith found Dr Kenny Bean in the staff canteen at the hospital. He was sitting on his own reading a book.

"Morning, doc," Smith said. "What are you reading?"

"The same sentence over and over again." Dr Bean looked up. "A particularly poignant one. 'When one person suffers from a delusion, it is called insanity. When many people suffer from a delusion it is called a Religion.' How poetically simple is that? You really should read this book."

"Zen and the Art of Motorcycle Maintenance," Smith read the cover. "I'm not really into motorcycles."

"It's more of a philosophical journey," Kenny told him. "What can I do for you?"

"Is there somewhere we can talk in private?"

"Sounds ominous. We can go through to my office."

"What's this all about?" Dr Bean closed the door of his office and sat down opposite Smith.

"Dr Lillian Marx," Smith got straight to the point. "How much do you know about her?"

"Enough," Dr Bean replied. "Why do you ask?"

"Something in my gut is telling me there's more to her than meets the eye."

"She came highly recommended – she's more than qualified and she's proven herself to be an asset to the team in the short time she's been here. What exactly is going on here?"

Smith told him about Matt McLean, and the press conference.

"And just because Dr Marx was seen chatting to your blast from the past, you think there's something sinister about her?" Kenny Bean said when Smith had finished.

"And somebody was following me this morning," Smith added. "This whole business has something to do with someone I know."

"I think you're barking up the wrong tree with Lillian," Dr Bean said. "Anyway, if you're so worried, why don't you just ask her? There's probably a perfectly innocent explanation."

He picked up the phone on his desk and pressed a button.

"Lillian. Are you in the building?"

Smith waited as Dr Bean mumbled a few *OK's* and *I see's.* He replaced the handset and turned to Smith. "She's at the snake centre in Clifton. She does some volunteer work there every now and again."

* * *

Smith parked in the tiny car park outside the brand new snake centre in Clifton, just outside the city centre. He didn't even know there was a snake centre in York. He walked past the high definition photographs of various species of snakes on the walls and approached a small reception desk.

"I'm looking for Doctor Marx," he told the long-haired man sitting behind the desk.

"She's busy in the milking lab," the man informed him.

"Where's that?"

"You're not allowed in there. We do have poisonous snakes here you know."

"I know," Smith took out his ID and put it in front of the man's face. "That's why I'm here."

Dr Lillian Marx looked exhausted when Smith found her in what was known as *the milking lab*. She had dark rings under her eyes and her hair looked unwashed. She was leaning over something on a glass table. A short man with black hair was also taking a keen interest in what was on the table. Dr Marx had her hand on the man's shoulder. It appeared to Smith to be more than just a friendly gesture. She pulled the man closer towards her and hugged him tightly. He looked up, and on seeing Smith standing there, he wiped his eyes and walked across the room and sat down in front of a laptop computer.

Dr Lillian Marx turned around and smiled at Smith. "We lost a Rattler. It was just a baby too. Is there something I can help you with?"

"Can we talk in private?" Smith asked her.

"There's a canteen. We can talk there."

Smith didn't notice, but the teary-eyed man turned and watched them leave. And when he was sure they couldn't see him, he stuck out his tongue.

Dr Marx sat down next to Smith. "I was just about to make my way to the station. I've had a lot to do here, and I've probably had five hours sleep in the past four days. What can I help you with?"

"How do you know Matt McLean?" Smith asked.

"Matt McLean?" she repeated. "I don't think I know... Oh, Matthew? I know him from my time in Australia. Do you know Matthew?"

"Very well. We grew up in the same town. What were you two talking about at the press conference?"

"What's all this about?" Dr Marx said.

"Matt McLean is the brother of a woman I was very close to. She's dead now, and Matt blames me for her death. He threatened me a while ago and I'm starting to think that this venom business is him making good on that threat."

"You can't be serious?"

"Deadly. How exactly did you and him meet? You said you spent time in Australia working with snakes. What's Matt McLean got to do with snakes?"

"He's a trader," Dr Marx explained. "He deals in exotic reptiles – predominantly snakes."

"Is that even legal?"

"You need a license," Dr Marx told him. "And there are certain species that cannot be bought and sold, but it's totally above board."

"What is he doing in York?" Smith asked.

"Business I assume. Are you honestly suggesting he's responsible for the envenomations?"

"He's in town, and he deals in exotic snakes. And he made it quite clear, last time we met that he was going to pay me back for the death of his sister. Do you know where he's staying?"

"DS Smith," Dr Marx said. "I barely know the man. Our paths crossed a few times up in Queensland. I was involved in research into a new anti-venom for the Coastal Taipan, and Matthew was conducting some business there. That's all there is to it. We exchanged a few words of greeting at the press conference and that's all."

"I'm sorry to have to ask you all this," Smith said. "But I just needed to know. I'm heading back to the station now. Do you need a lift?"

"I need to go home to shower and change first," she told him. "I'll see you there in about an hour."

CHAPTER THIRTY THREE

Smith got into his car and was about to turn the key in the ignition when his mobile phone started to ring.

"Smith," he answered it.

"Detective Sergeant Jason Smith?" a man asked.

"That's right. Who is this?"

"Phil Davies. York Gazette. We've met a few times before."

Smith vaguely recalled the name. If could remember correctly, Phil Davies was one of a rare breed of journalists – he possessed integrity.

"What can I do for you?" he asked.

"It's more what I can do for you," Davies told him. "I had an interesting phone call earlier this morning. You do realise I am jeopardizing a potentially huge story here."

"I appreciate it," Smith said. "Go on."

"A man called the paper and told me you'd omitted some crucial information at the press conference yesterday. Some kind of correspondence at the murder scenes with your phone number on it."

Smith could feel the blood pumping in his temples. The only people who knew about the letters at the crime scenes were the members of his team. And the killer.

"Do you know who phoned you?" Smith asked. "Did he leave a name?"

"He called himself BB. And there's something else. He told me there will be another one tomorrow. A particularly quick one he said. Then there will be one more and then it will stop. Those were his exact words."

"Do you think he was telling the truth?"

""Was your phone number on the correspondence at the crime scene?" Davies asked.

"Yes."

"Then what do you think?"

"Do you remember anything else about the phone call? What did he talk like?"

"He was very articulate. But he had a very odd way of speaking."

"Like an accent? An Australian accent perhaps?"

"No," Davies said. "He was definitely not Australian. His sentence construction was very strange, that's all, and he had a lisp."

"A lisp?"

"It wasn't that apparent at first but it came out towards the end of the conversation."

Smith knew for a fact that Matt McLean didn't speak with a lisp.

He suddenly thought of something.

"The man who called," he said. "Did he phone on your mobile or a landline?"

"He got through to the switchboard at the paper."

"Then we ought to be able to trace the number he phoned from."

"Easily," Davies agreed. "I'll get hold of the telephone company and send the information straight through."

"Thank you," Smith said. "I really appreciate you calling. Could you do me one massive favour though?"

"I'm not going to run with the story if that's what you're thinking. I must be losing my touch, but I understand how this would be for you if the public found out about it."

It was normally a ten minute drive from Clifton to the station but Smith managed it in five. His heart was pumping so quickly by the time he arrived he had to take a few deep breaths before he got out of the car. He rushed inside and headed straight for Brownhill's office. He knocked on the door and went in. The DI was looking at something on her laptop.

"Well?" she looked up at him. "You've found something, haven't you? I know that expression."

Smith sat down opposite her. "A man phoned the Gazette this morning with information about the murders. He mentioned my phone number."

"But we didn't give out that information," Brownhill said.

"Exactly, so either it was someone on our team – which I very much doubt, or it was the murderer. The bloke I spoke to, Phil Davies is going to send through the number he called on."

"Well I've seen it all now," Brownhill said. "Why didn't he just use the information and run with it?"

"Journalistic integrity?"

"An oxymoron if ever there was one. Do we know anything else about this mystery caller?"

"He had an odd way of talking. And he had a lisp."

"Of course he didn't leave a name?"

"He called himself BB, but that's probably not going to help us. He won't be using his real name."

Whitton and Yang Chu came in the room. Smith told them about his conversation with the journalist from the Gazette.

"We think we might have found Matt McLean," Whitton said. "We checked arrivals and he came in on a Quantas flight a week ago."

"Just before the venom killing started," Smith pointed out. "You said you found him?"

"We've found where he's staying," Yang Chu said. "But he's not there at the moment. He owns a house here."

"Why would he buy a house in York?" Smith asked.

"I don't know, but it all seems to be legit. He's on the electoral role – he pays his council tax, and the title deeds are in his real name. If he is our snake venom murderer, he's hardly trying to stay under the radar."

"I'll need that address," Smith said.

His phoned pinged to tell him he'd received a message. He opened it up. It was from Phil Davies of the York Gazette. Smith read the message and sighed.

"This is the number of the man who phoned the York Gazette this morning," he said. "It's a public phone. The bastard phoned from a public phone on Swale Street."

"At least we know he's in town," Yang Chu said.

"He told Davies there's going to be two more," Smith said. "We need to find him before that happens. And we need to make the public aware."

"What are you suggesting?" Brownhill said.

"I'm suggesting we warn people about suspicious hand-written packages."

"You do realise what that will involve? And you do also realise that warning the general public will not only cause mass panic, but it will contradict what you told them at the press conference. This isn't going to make us look very good."

"Right now, I couldn't care less. If we can save two lives, it's a price worth paying. I want a press release issued before the mail gets delivered in the morning. Yang Chu, get hold of the liaison officer and get it done."

Yang Chu looked at Brownhill, and the DI nodded her approval.

CHAPTER THIRTY FOUR

Smith parked his car outside the address Yang Chu had given him for Matt McLean and he and Whitton got out. The house was at the end of a row of Edwardian terraces. It was a three storey building which appeared to be well maintained.

"These places are not cheap," Whitton said.

"Matt McLean is not exactly short of cash," Smith reminded her. "He inherited Lucy's millions remember. Why would he buy such a big house in a town he doesn't live in all the time? It doesn't make sense. Let's see if he's at home, shall we?"

They walked the short distance from the road to the front door and Smith pressed the bell. He waited a couple of seconds then banged on the door.

"It doesn't look like he's home," Whitton said.

Smith banged on the door again, bent down and looked through the letterbox. There was no indication that anybody was inside the house. There was an alleyway that ran down the side of the building. Smith walked its entire length and jumped over the small fence at the back of the house. He peered through the large window into the living room. The room was very sparsely furnished – there were two single-seater couches and a sideboard in the corner. That was all.

Smith looked through the glass in the back door. The kitchen door opened onto a wide hallway that ran towards the front door. An impressive wooden staircase stood to the right. Smith realised there was something strange about the staircase. It didn't stop in the hallway – it carried on further down. The house obviously had a basement.

"What are you doing?" a voice was heard behind Smith and he jumped. It was Whitton. "What exactly are you looking for?"

"I don't know. This place has a basement."

"Most of these old houses do," Whitton told him.

"Why would someone who spends hardly any time in a place want a house with a basement? Unless they're up to something and they don't want people to know what."

"Loads of people have basements. Maybe he's using it for storage."

"There's nothing in the house, Whitton," Smith said. "Why would he need storage space? I'm going to have a look inside."

"You're going to break in? Are you mad? You could lose your job."

"No one will ever know. There's a set of keys hanging next to the door inside. Keep an eye out round the front for me. Park the car a bit further up the road so as not to look suspicious."

The back door was old, and the putty around the glass panes was cracked and blistered. In some places there was no putty at all. Smith scraped at the edge of one of the panes of glass and managed to remove enough putty to loosen the window. He wiggled it from side to side until it came away from the door altogether and fell to the kitchen floor with a crash. Smith reached inside and found the set of keys hanging on the hook. There were three of them. The second one he tried opened up the back door.

He stepped over the broken glass on the floor and made his way out of the kitchen and into the hallway. There was a strange sound coming from somewhere in the house – a low buzzing noise that he couldn't quite place. He stopped and listened. The buzzing sound appeared to be coming from the basement. Smith walked slowly down the wooden staircase and stopped in front of a metal door. He pushed open the door and was hit by an oppressive wave of foul-smelling hot air.

The room was well lit and when Smith stepped inside he realised what was making the low buzzing noise. Two boilers were pumping out heat on the far side of the room. There were glass containers on a desk that ran the whole length of one wall. A pile of packing crates was stacked up against the opposite wall. There was a small refrigerator standing on a table next to the crates. Smith opened the door and gasped. Inside were rows of medical vials. Syringes of all different sizes lay on the shelf below, still in their plastic packaging. He walked over to the containers lying on the desk and peered inside one of them. It appeared to be empty apart from a large white rock on a layer of sand on the bottom and a thick tree branch running from one corner of the container to the other. On the top of the container was a label that read 'Mole Snake.' Smith spotted something at the bottom of the rock. Something was moving. He put his face to the glass to get a better look when his mobile phone started to ring.

Whitton shivered in the passenger seat of Smith's car. The heater hadn't worked for months now and the icy wind outside had now lowered the temperature in the old Ford Sierra to just above freezing. She looked at the clock on the dashboard for the third time in a minute. Smith was taking too long inside the house. Matt McLean could come home at any minute. She heard the sound of a car engine and turned around. A small van with the name 'Franklin Security Services' on it was driving up the road towards her. The van passed by and stopped outside Matt McLean's house. Whitton took out her phone.

"There's someone outside," she told Smith. "It looks like a security company. You must have triggered a silent alarm. Get out of there now."

"The basement is full of snakes," Smith told her. "And there's a fridge full of what looks to be vials of poison. We've got the bastard."

"Get out of there. We've got nothing if you get caught breaking and entering."

Smith knew that Whitton was right. Anything he found inside the house would be inadmissible due to his unorthodox method of obtaining it. He closed the steel door behind him and started to climb the stairs up to the ground floor. He could hear voices coming from outside the house. He headed for the kitchen – he would leave the same way he came in. He had just reached the back door when he heard a familiar voice.

"What the hell are you doing in my house?"

CHAPTER THIRTY FIVE

"What the hell are you doing in my house?" Matt McLean asked Smith again. Two men in security guard's uniform stood behind him. Smith thought hard about how he was going to explain the situation.

He took out his ID. "DS Smith," he spoke to the security guards. "I was looking for Mr McLean when I noticed his back window had been smashed and the back door was wide open so I went in and had a look."

"Do you know this man, sir?" one of the guards asked Matt.

"We go way back," Matt replied. "I think you can leave now. I'll make sure I get the window fixed."

Whitton appeared. "Is everything alright?"

"Everything's fine," Matt replied.

"Let's go inside," Smith suggested. "It's freezing out here."

"I'll ask you again," Matt McLean said. "What were you doing in my house?"

He, Smith and Whitton sat at the table in the kitchen.

"Following up on a gut feeling," Smith replied. "And I think it's you who ought to be answering questions right now. What are you doing with snakes in your basement?"

Matt started to laugh. It took Smith completely by surprise.

"Sorry," Matt said. "This is about the snake venom thing isn't it? I read about it online."

"What do you know about it?"

"Do you think I had something to do with it?" Matt asked.

"Do you? How do you explain the snakes in the basement?"

"Come with me," Matt stood up and walked down the hallway. "I want to show you something."

Smith and Whitton followed behind him.

"He could be up to something," Whitton whispered. "Shouldn't we call for back-up?"

"I don't think that will be necessary," Smith said.

Matt led them down the staircase towards the basement. They stopped in front of the metal door. Matt opened it and gestured for them to go inside.

"Whitton," Smith said. "You stay out here."

"As you wish," Matt said and went inside the stuffy room.

"Why is this room full of snakes?" Smith asked him. "Where did they all come from?"

"From all over the world. This is what I do, Jason. I import and export reptiles. I have all the necessary permits and licenses."

"Why York of all places?" Smith said.

"It's central. It's not far from London, and it's a hell of a lot cheaper to work from here than it is in the capital. Here I'm close to Eastern Europe where the new money is. And where there's new money there's always a demand for products such as mine."

"Why on earth would a person want to buy a poisonous snake?"

"To impress. Any fool can own a dog or a cat, but if you mention in passing in a business meeting you own a couple of rattlesnakes, you will gain respect. Do you want to see them?"

Smith didn't really want to see them but he needed to check if any of the snakes were the same as the snakes that were responsible for the deaths of three people.

"I have two Whip snakes coming in," Matt told Smith. "I had to get a special permit for those. Most of the ones I've got now are not really harmful." He stopped next to one of the containers. "Except this little beauty. It's not called the Death Adder for nothing. Do you want to have a closer look?"

"No thanks." Smith remembered what he'd seen in the fridge. "Do you take their venom? Do you milk them?"

"No. It's too much effort for too little return. I bring the snakes here and ship them out when the deal's done. It's all above board. The snakes are well looked after. You've probably noticed how warm it is in here – they're cold-blooded animals and they would die if it were any colder. They get fed, and they're handled carefully."

He walked over to the fridge and Smith was instantly on his guard. He knew what was stored inside. He stepped back towards the door, ready to run if he had to.

"Like I said," Matt opened the door of the refrigerator. "Everything here is perfectly in order. This is where I keep my store of anti-venom. It's all up to date. You can check."

"What do you need anti-venom for?"

"For when I have to handle the snakes. It's very rare but accidents do happen, and people who handle snakes do get bitten every once in a while. I have the anti-venom on hand should that happen. Did you really believe I had something to do with killing those people?"

"It all seemed to fit," Smith said. "You happened to arrive in the country just before this started – the line of business you're in, and the fact that the last time we spoke you issued a veiled threat."

"I did what?"

"That night in the pub. You told me you blamed me entirely for Lucy's death and it was far from over."

"Did I really say that? I can't remember saying that? Was I drunk?"

"Very."

"Then I apologise. I had a bit of a problem. I don't drink anymore because of it."

Matt McLean had just about managed to convince Smith he had nothing to do with the venom killings but he still needed to be one hundred percent certain.

"You arrived at Heathrow last week?" he said.

"That's right," Matt said. "Last week Wednesday."

"And have you been in York the whole time since then?"

"I spent Monday and Tuesday night down in London. I had a client to see. I drove back up here yesterday."

"I assume you have witnesses who can corroborate this?"

"Of course. I also have proof of credit card transactions on both Monday and Tuesday. Is there anything else I can do for you? I have quite a lot to organise. I have a rich Latvian client who needs a Herald Snake delivered in time for Christmas. It's a present for his daughter."

"What's wrong with a good old-fashioned Barbie Doll?" Smith said. "That's all for now. I might need to speak to you again though."

"Any time." Matt handed him one of his cards. "Phone first and I'll let you in through the front door this time."

Smith smiled. "Sorry about the window."

"I've never liked that back door," Matt smiled. "I was thinking of replacing it anyway."

CHAPTER THIRTY SIX

"Well that's Matt McLean ruled out then," Smith said to Whitton as they drove. "He's got an alibi for when two out of three of the envelopes were posted. He was down in London. And his snake business is legit – he showed me the documents to prove it. Damn it. I was sure we had him."

"What about the threat he made?" Whitton asked.

"He reckons he can't even remember saying it."

"Who in their right mind would want to buy a snake?" Whitton mused.

"That's what I asked. But it appears to be quite a lucrative game to be in."

"What's the plan now then?"

"I'm afraid I don't have one. The press release is going to make our lives hell until we catch this maniac."

"Do you think we will catch him?"

"I don't know. How do you catch a murderer who makes sure he isn't at the scene of the murder?"

"Motive," Whitton said.

"The only motive I've come up with is someone who wants to hurt me, Erica, and I still can't think of who that could be. I've lost count of how many people I've pissed off over the years, but I haven't pissed anybody off enough to justify this."

* * *

"Let's recap what we have," DI Brownhill said.

The team was gathered once more in the small conference room at the station.

"We can rule out Matt McLean," Smith said. "He runs a legitimate business and he has an alibi for the times two of the envelopes were posted."

"What about Dr Marx?" Yang Chu asked. "Did she explain how she knows McLean?"

"She met him a couple of times up in Northern Australia," Smith told him. "They hardly know each other. That's all there is to it."

"Maybe she was the one who posted the envelopes for McLean," Yang Chu suggested. "That would make his alibi irrelevant wouldn't it?"

"It's not Dr Marx," Bridge said.

"You're just saying that because you're in love," Yang Chu said.

"That's enough," Smith could feel a headache coming on. "None of the snakes in Matt McLean's basement are the same as the ones responsible for killing those people."

"What about the man who phoned the newspaper this morning?" Whitton said. "Do we know any more about him?"

"Only that he goes by the name of BB and he speaks with a lisp. He called from a public phone and as far as we know he hasn't tried to contact the press again."

"Which brings us to the press release," Brownhill said. "The press liaison officer has issued a release and it will be live in an hour or so. We need to prepare ourselves for a backlash. It is not going to be pleasant."

"Can I see it before it goes live?" Smith asked.

"What for?"

"Because I'm the one who's going to be facing the firing squad, boss. I'd quite like to make sure Walker gets all the facts right."

"Our press liaison officer is one of the best. He'll have got the facts right. He's exceptionally good at his job."

"So am I," Smith stood up. "But even I've been known to fuck up every once in a while."

He exited the small conference room, leaving a team of wide-eyed detectives in his wake.

Neil Walker was getting ready to leave for the day when Smith went in his office.

"Press release is done," he said. "I've scheduled it to go live in time for the evening press to air it. And I managed to get hold of the local TV station. They've agreed to run a piece about the potentially dangerous envelopes. Hopefully, the whole of York will catch it. Is there something I can help you with?"

"I want to read the release before it goes out," Smith told him.

"Of course. I haven't shut down my laptop." His hand danced around the keypad and then stopped. "There you go. Take a seat."

The press release was concise and to the point. Neil Walker did know what he was doing and he'd done a good job.

"Do you know Phil Davies from the Gazette?" Smith asked when he'd finished reading.

"I've known Phil for years. One of the good guys."

"Can you make sure he gets the press release before the rest of them?"

"I can," Walker replied. "But why do you want me to do that?"

"Because Phil Davies is one of the good guys. Thanks. You can get off home now."

Dusk was close as Smith walked into the canteen. The last rays of sunlight were moving quickly away from the spires of the Minster in the distance. Smith really felt like a beer, but he knew that coffee would be a better idea right now. He selected the strongest the machine had to offer and took the coffee down to his office. Whitton came in a few moments later.

"What was that all about?" she sat behind his desk. "The DI is spitting fire. She's only going to let you get away with outbursts like that for so long you know."

"She loves me really. And I just wanted to make sure Walker had the press release spot on. This is important."

"Why do you have to take on everything yourself? You're going to burn out if you carry on like this, and I'd quite like to hang on to my husband for a bit longer."

"I can't help it. And I needed to know it was right before it was released."

"And was it?"

"It was excellent. Walker worded it in such a way there can be no danger of misinterpretation."

"There you go then," Whitton got up, stood behind Smith and began to rub his shoulders.

"Let's go home," he turned around and kissed his wife on the lips. "I'm knackered and I don't think we're going to achieve anything more today." He placed his hand in hers and they walked out of the office, leaving the strong coffee unfinished on the desk.

CHAPTER THIRTY SEVEN

The man with the lisp was pacing up and down his living room. He'd been pacing up and down for the last half an hour. The heating in his house was turned up as high as it could go and yet the man shivered. He sat down on the sofa and wrapped his hands around the cup of tea on the coffee table. So far everything had gone according to plan. It had been smoother sailing than he thought it would be, but now he had a problem. A problem in the shape of an Australian called Matthew McLean.

He'd kept a close eye on McLean and up until now he hadn't been any cause for concern.

But now all that had changed.

The man with the lisp had seen him talking to Detective Sergeant Jason Smith, and that could only spell trouble. Matthew McLean could ruin everything. Not only did he know the identity of the man with the lisp – he knew where he operated from, and where he was likely to be at any given moment. It wasn't clear whether he would be able to put the pieces together and reveal the truth but the man with the lisp simply couldn't afford to take that risk.

Not when he was so close.

He unlocked the door to the modified cellar and checked the thermostat on the wall. The ambient temperature was just right – his *lovelies* could sleep well. He locked the door behind him, put on a thick overcoat and left the house.

His black hatchback was covered with a fine coating of frost when he got inside. The temperatures were set to drop way below freezing during the night. The man with the lisp turned the key in the ignition and hoped the little black car would start. On the third turn of the key the engine purred to life and the heater came on inside the car.

* * *

Matt McLean closed the metal door that led to the basement and walked up the stairs. He'd fed his snakes and they were snug in their glass cages for the night. One of the heaters had stopped working, but Matt had managed to cover the cages with blankets to insulate them for the night. He would get the heater fixed tomorrow. He went through to the kitchen, got a beer out of the fridge and took it with him to the living room.

One beer won't hurt, he thought.

Earlier in the year, Matt had developed what most doctors would term a serious alcohol dependence, and he'd found himself in a catch-22 situation: when he was drinking he turned into an obnoxious, argumentative thug, and when he wasn't drinking, the craving for alcohol made him even more obstreperous. He'd woken up one day after a particularly vicious bender and, with a strength of character that surprised him, he'd decided enough was enough. He hadn't touched a drop since.

Until now.

Matt turned on the television. The news was about to begin. He took a small sip of the beer and smiled. He'd forgotten how good it tasted. He very rarely watched the local news, but he was interested to see if there would be anything about the recent snake venom murders. The opening credits came on and Matt's doorbell chimed in the hallway.

"Damn it," he cursed. "Who the hell is calling at this hour?"

He put his beer down and went to answer the door.

The man standing on the doorstep was a man Matt hadn't seen for quite some time, and if he were to be honest it was a man he hoped he wouldn't have to see again.

"Boris," he said. "What are you doing here?"

The man glanced behind him and shivered. "Can I come in? I need a favour."

Matt gestured for him to come inside and closed the door behind them.
"What's this favour?"

"I have a client looking for a specific specimen," the man called Boris said.
The last two words in the sentence sounded almost comical due to his lisp.

"I was about to watch the news," Matt told him. "Do you mind?"

"I'll watch it with you."

The local news presenter had just started with the report on the venom
killings. She outlined what had already been spoken about at the press
conference. Matt McLean's guest watched with keen interest, but his facial
expression changed dramatically when a close-up of an A4 sized envelope
appeared on the screen. The name and address had been purposefully
blurred to protect the identity of the victim, but Boris knew.

It was his handwriting on the envelope.

The news presenter went on to warn the public about the potentially
deadly consequences of these envelopes and advised anyone receiving
anything like them to contact the police immediately. A telephone number
appeared on the screen shortly afterwards. It was the number for the
switchboard of York Police.

Another image appeared on the screen. It was a piece of paper, and this
time the words written on it were perfectly clear.

"This is terrible," Matt said.

"Despicable," Boris agreed.

On the piece of paper was the note the first victim, Frank Broadbent had
received.

"Black Mamba?" Matt exclaimed as he read it.

Smith's mobile number had been crossed out at the bottom of the page, but
the presenter continued to elaborate. She reported that the note contained
the number of the detective leading the investigation into the snake venom
murders, and the police were looking for any information about who the

mystery sender could be. The number for the switchboard remained on the screen the whole time.

"What was this favour?" Matt asked when the report was finished and a story about a local hockey team came on.

"Like I said," Boris said. "I have a client looking for a certain asp."

"Go on."

"A Death Adder."

"My Death Adder is already sold," Matt told him. "I'll be shipping her out in the new year. I'm afraid I can't help you."

"Oh, I have a Death Adder, what I don't have is any anti-venom. My client insisted that part of the agreement was that anti-venom be delivered with the snake. I can pay anything you ask."

Matt tried to think quickly. He did have the anti-venom for that particular snake, and his Death Adder wasn't due to be delivered until after the new year, and he could always acquire more. Besides, he didn't like the man sitting next to him, and if all it took was a vial of anti-venom to get rid of him it was a small price to pay.

"I've got some in the basement," he said.

Matt opened the door of the basement and switched on the light.

"It's too cold in here," Boris observed.

"One of the heaters isn't working properly," Matt told him. "I'll get someone out to look at it tomorrow, but in the meantime I've wrapped blankets around the cages."

"It's probably just the thermostat. I've lost count of how many of these I've fixed. Those blankets won't be much help when the temperature drops tonight. Do you want me to have a look?"

Without waiting for Matt to reply, he walked over to the heater, took out a small pocket knife and opened up the front cover.

"There's your problem," he undid the tiny screw attached to a wire that had come loose, pushed the wire back through and tightened it again. The heater came to life with a loud hum.

"These things are old," he said. "And they just need looking after. The anti-venom?"

"Of course," Matt approached the small refrigerator and opened it up. "Acanthophis Antarcticus."

He'd found what he was looking for. He took out the vial and handed it to Boris.

"Invoice me what you consider it to be worth," Boris placed it inside the pocket of his overcoat. "I will pay anything."

Matt did some mental arithmetic. The anti-venom hadn't actually cost him anything – it had been part of a deal he'd made more than enough out of anyway.

"Consider it payment for fixing the heater."

The temperature in the basement had already risen three or four degrees.

"Deal," Boris smiled. "And now we'd better remove these blankets. You don't want to fry your babies now, do you?"

They set about unwrapping the thick blankets from the glass cages. They had almost finished when Boris stopped next to one of them.

"I forgot to ask. Do you have a syringe? The Death Adder has to leave first thing in the morning, I've run out of syringes and there will be nowhere open to buy one so early tomorrow."

"I'll get one for you."

Matt opened up the fridge once more and reached inside for a plastic-wrapped syringe. He heard an almighty crash behind him and turned around. One of the glass containers was smashed to pieces on the floor. He watched as Boris picked up what was inside the container and with astonishing speed rushed towards him.

The snake with the longest fangs of all the Australian snakes had its mouth wide open. Matt raised his hand, but he was not quick enough. The man with the lisp released his grip on the Death Adder's neck and let it strike. The fangs closed around Matt McLean's neck and he screamed as he felt them pierce the skin. The pain was unbelievable but Matt's brain was concentrating on something much more serious than excruciating pain. He knew what the venom of a Death Adder could do.

And he had just handed over the only anti-venom he had that would counteract the poison.

The neurotoxic properties of the snakes were already attacking his central nervous system. Very soon, he would lose feeling in his extremities, followed by muscles. Death would come when the toxin reached his organs. His heart would stop beating, and blood would stop flowing.

Matt knew he might still have a chance if he could only manage to overpower the man with the lisp and raise the alarm. He felt the fangs of the snake release their grip on his neck as they were yanked out, ripping flesh in the process, and he fell to the ground. He watched as Boris took out a small sack from his overcoat and gently placed the snake inside. He tied the top of the sack and smiled at Matt.

"Does it hurt?"

"Please give me the anti-venom," Matt pleaded. "You don't have to do this."

"It won't hurt for much longer. I'll stay for a while to make sure it stops hurting."

"Why are you doing this?" Matt could feel that his arms and legs were becoming weaker and weaker by the second.

He tried to get up but his legs were no longer working. He could feel his pulse quickening and he tried to take a few deep breaths to slow it down but it was getting harder and harder to breathe. The last thing he saw was the man with the lisp standing in the doorway. He turned off the light and left the room, slamming the metal door behind him.

CHAPTER THIRTY EIGHT

"What do you think is going to happen now?" Whitton asked Smith.
They had just finished watched the local TV news report on the venom
murders.

"I think tomorrow is going to be a long day," Smith replied. "I bet the
switchboard is already going crazy. I'm starting to wonder if this was such a
good idea after all."

"It was the only thing we could do. We've run out of ideas. Hopefully enough
people have been warned about these envelopes."

"How's Laura?" Smith decided to change the subject.

Laura had been ill – she'd been taken out of daycare and Whitton had
thought it best that she stayed with her parents with everything that had
gone on in the past week.

"I spoke to my Mum earlier," she said. "Laura is much better, and my Mum
and Dad love having her around. They've offered to have her for the whole
weekend."

"Your folks are great," Smith said. "I don't know what we'd do without
them."

"We can spoil them at Christmas. I'm really looking forward to spending a
few days off over Christmas without having to worry about work. I've
already put in some leave – I've done my bit over the years."

"I suppose I ought to put in for a few days leave too. That's if this venom
thing is over by then."

"It will be. Now, let's talk about something else. Or we could watch a DVD."

"Only if I can choose. You always pick some chick-flick, fall asleep ten
minutes into it and make me suffer for the rest of the film."

* * *

Whitton wasn't wrong about the switchboard at the station going crazy. The news report had aired less than an hour earlier and they'd already received over two hundred calls. Brownhill had decided it would be a good idea for members of the investigation team to help out – they would be in a better position to spot the hoax calls and time-wasters, and it had been Bridge and Yang Chu who had drawn the short straw.

Thirty minutes in and Bridge had already had enough.

"I'm knackered. I need a break," he told Yang Chu. "I didn't bust my arse to become a DS so I could spend all night answering the bloody phone."

"You didn't bust your arse," Yang Chu reminded him. "You only got the gig because you'd been here longer than me."

"You didn't bust your arse, Sarge, if you don't mind. Anyway, I need coffee if I'm going to make it through the night."

"Get me one too will you?" Yang Chu said, and then added, "Sarge."

"Cheeky bastard," Bridge mumbled and headed upstairs to the canteen.

Yang Chu ended the call and sighed as the light in front of him indicated there was another one waiting. It was going to be a long night. So far they hadn't had one piece of information that could help. The majority of the calls were concerned residents asking irrelevant questions.

What should they do in the event of being injected with snake venom?

Were the local hospitals stocking up on anti-venom as a precaution?

One man had even asked if it was necessary to block off his letter box.

Yang Chu pressed the button. "York Police. How can I help you?"

"You can't," it was a man's voice. "It's more about how I can help you."

Yang Chu didn't know why, but there was something different about this caller, something he couldn't put his finger on. "How can you help us?"

"I know who you are looking for. Your *venom murderer* as the press have so eloquently labelled him. I know where he is."

"Could I please have your name, sir?"

"Not yet. All in good time."

"Sir," Yang Chu said. "What is it you want to tell me? I have another call waiting."

"Do you know what a krait is?"

"It's a wooden container. Please, sir, if you have nothing pertaining to this investigation, could you hang up now."

"A krait is a snake responsible for more than ten thousand fatalities in India each year. There is no anti-venom. Are you still listening?"

"Yes," Yang Chu said. "What do you want to tell me?"

The line went dead.

Bridge returned with the coffee. "Anything happening?"

"More than the fair share of nutters this time," Yang Chu told him. "But I've just got off a call with a bloke who sounded quite genuine."

"Did he leave a name?"

"He just mentioned something about a snake I've never heard of and hung up. Hold on."

All of the phone calls were being recorded. Yang Chu played the most recent call again.

"Play that again," Bridge said. "There's something about the voice."

Yang Chu did as he was asked.

"Did you hear his lisp?" Bridge said when the line went dead on the recording. "He spoke with a lisp. The man who phoned the Gazette spoke with a lisp. I think you've just spoken to our killer."

* * *

Smith was contemplating turning off the film he wasn't even watching when his phone started to ring in the kitchen. Whitton was snoring softly on the sofa next to him. More raucous noises were coming from Fred and Theakston. The Bull Terrier and the gruesome Pug were engaged in the snorting competition of a lifetime and it wasn't quite clear who was winning.

Smith left them to it and went to see who was phoning him at this time of night. He sighed when he saw DI Brownhill's number come up on the screen. "Boss," he answered it.

"There's been a development from the calls coming in to the switchboard," Brownhill told him. "Yang Chu took a call a short while ago, we've listened to the recording and it appears to be genuine. It came from a man with a lisp who appeared to know quite a bit about snakes."

"Did you manage to trace the call?"

"Let me finish. The call was made from a landline. A local number. That number is listed to a Matthew McLean."

"Are you sure?" Smith asked.

"Positive. We've got an address and we're about to make our way there now."

"I'm on my way," Smith said and rang off.

CHAPTER THIRTY NINE

It was almost midnight when Smith stopped outside the house he had broken into earlier that day. He spotted Yang Chu's Ford Focus further up the street. The lights were on inside the house and the flickering of a TV set could be seen through the thin curtains. Smith walked up to where Yang Chu had parked. Brownhill was sitting in the passenger seat. Smith got in the back.

"What's the plan?" he said.

"Back-up is on the way," Brownhill told him. "They should be here shortly. We'll wait until they get here before we go in."

"This is all wrong, boss. Something doesn't feel right here."

"A call was made from a landline registered to this address," Brownhill reminded him.

"What exactly did the caller say?" Smith addressed the question to Yang Chu.

"Something about knowing who we're looking for," Yang Chu told him. "Then he asked if I knew what a krait was."

"It's a highly venomous snake. What else?"

"That was about it. And he spoke with a lisp like the bloke who phoned the York Gazette."

"Matt McLean doesn't have a lisp," Smith said. "He's never had a lisp. Something isn't right."

"We'll see," Brownhill said.

Two police cars approached and parked behind them. Their lights were off.

"Let's go," Brownhill said and got out of the car.

Smith did the same. Bridge walked up with three PCs.

"Looks like we've got the bastard," Bridge said. "The lights are on in the house, so he's still there."

"Don't get your hopes up," Smith took out a cigarette and lit it. "It's not Matt McLean. I spoke to him earlier, remember. He was out of town for two of the murders and why would he be stupid enough to phone the switchboard using his landline?"

"Maybe he doesn't know we can trace the call?" Yang Chu said.

"This killer has orchestrated three perfect murders so far," Smith reminded them. "He phoned the Gazette from a public phone, remember."

"We're going in," Brownhill said. "Smith, you, Bridge and myself will go in the front. Yang Chu, you and uniform can stay at the back in case he tries to escape that way. Let's go."

Smith went first. His gut was telling him that this was a complete waste of time. He placed his hand on the door and pushed. The door was open. The sound of the television could be heard from the living room. The lights were on in all the rooms downstairs. There was a cordless telephone on the table in the hallway that Smith hadn't noticed when he'd been there earlier.

"I'll check upstairs," Bridge whispered and crept up the wooden staircase.

Smith went into the living room. The television was showing a repeat of a football game but nobody was watching it. Smith came out and made his way towards the kitchen. Brownhill followed closely behind him. Yang Chu was standing outside the back door. He was looking at the broken window.

"There's nobody upstairs," Bridge came in.

"It looks like there was a break-in," Yang Chu said through the gap in the window.

"It wasn't exactly a break-in," Smith told them about how he had managed to gain access to the house earlier.

"Is there anything else you're not telling us?" Brownhill said. "What were you thinking?"

"I was thinking we were running out of time, and I decided to act on my own initiative. And, yes, there is something else I haven't told you – this house has a basement."

Smith could feel the difference in temperature even before he opened the door that led to the basement. He pushed the metal door open and was met with a muggy darkness. He took out his phone and switched on the torch. He shone it around the room and let it rest on something on the floor. His heart quickened when he realised what it was. One of the glass containers that housed the snakes was smashed to pieces. Smith instinctively backed up a few feet. He remembered Matt McLean telling him that not all of the snakes he kept in here were dangerous, but Smith recalled the name of one of them.

Death Adder.

"Be careful," he turned to Brownhill and Bridge. "One of the snake containers has been broken. The snake could still be around here somewhere."

Brownhill nodded, but Bridge didn't stick around. Smith had never seen him move so quickly – he made it up to the top of the staircase and was out of the front door before Smith had a chance to say anything else. The beam of his torch found a light switch, Smith took out a tissue and used it to flick the light on.

Matt McLean was lying against the opposite wall by the heaters. His face was a disturbing blue colour, his eyes were open, but he didn't appear to be breathing. He had what appeared to be a deep laceration to his neck. The blood around the wound had turned black. Smith leaned over him and checked for a pulse. It was extremely weak but he was still alive.

"We need an ambulance here right now," Smith shouted. "Matt," he kneeled down. "We're going to get you out of here. There's an ambulance on the way."

Matt McLean's mouth started to quiver. Smith put his hand on his shoulder. Despite the heat in the room, the shoulder felt cold and clammy.

"Bris," Matt said.

Spittle was running down his cheek.

"Don't try to speak," Smith said. "You'll be alright. The ambulance is almost here."

Matt shook his head, and from the expression on his face, Smith could see he was in extreme agony. His eyes stared ahead wildly, and one side of his face was twitching.

"Where the hell is that ambulance?" Smith screamed to Brownhill.

The DI was still standing in the doorway.

"It's on the way," she said.

Smith turned back to the man he'd known since he was in primary school. A man whose sister, Smith had once loved. This was the man who had looked after Smith during his first few days in England all those years ago. Matt opened his mouth again, and, with an action that seemed to drain what little strength he had left, he reached out his arm and pulled Smith closer. He whispered something in Smith's ear, his eyes rolled back in his head and he exhaled one last weak breath.

CHAPTER FORTY

Smith sat on the wall outside Matt McLean's house smoking a cigarette. It was bitterly cold, but Smith didn't appear to notice. The ambulance had taken Matt's body away. It had arrived too late, and even if it had got there in time, he doubted if it would have made a difference. He finished his cigarette and lit another one. Grant Webber's car pulled up a few metres away and the head of forensics got out. He rubbed his hands together and walked up to Smith.

"Have you got one of those for me?" he pointed to Smith's cigarette.

Smith took out the packet and handed it to him. Webber only smoked when he was under stress, and Smith wasn't in the mood to ask him about it.

"What have we got in there?" the head of forensics asked.

"I'd say it's our first real crime scene. The dead man is called Matthew McLean. Thirty eight years old. Originally from Fremantle. He's been dealing in exotic snakes for a while. He keeps them in the basement."

"And it's definitely not a freak accident?"

"No. He did keep some venomous snakes, but he was prepared in the event of him being bitten. He kept an up-to-date store of anti-venom in the same room as the snakes. We wouldn't have even known he was here if we hadn't received a call from his landline. I'm almost certain our venom killer did this."

"That phone will be what we'll concentrate on first then," Webber threw his cigarette butt into the road and went inside the house.

Smith walked away from Matt McLean's house. The two words Matt had whispered in his ears before he died were still there, like echoes inside his head. It didn't make any sense.

Boris Boronov.

The first name meant nothing to Smith, but the name Boronov had haunted him for years. Viktor Boronov had done nothing but cause pain. He was the one who taken Smith's sister, thus affecting the direction his life was to take for years afterwards. Viktor Boronov was partly responsible for shaping Smith into the person he had turned out to be.

Viktor Boronov was dead – Whitton had put a scalpel through his heart, and he had been pronounced dead at the scene.

But who was this man who had suddenly appeared to cause more pain in Smith's life? A man with the name Boronov.

"Where have you been?" Brownhill asked Smith when he returned to the house.

"I needed a walk," Smith told her. "Matt McLean whispered something in my ear before he died. A name – Boris Boronov. That's the name of our venom murderer."

"Boris Boronov?" Brownhill repeated. "That's who BB is. Do you think he's related to Viktor Boronov?"

"What do you think, boss? He has to be. How many Boronovs have you met in your life?"

"OK. At least we have a name. Grant has almost finished inside. We'll lock up and tape up the house and I'll arrange for an expert to come and remove those snakes first thing tomorrow morning."

"Did that snake turn up?"

"Snake?"

"The one from the broken container? I just hope it doesn't jump out and bite somebody. You didn't appear too concerned back there. Did you see the way Bridge reacted?"

"I would have to assume DS Bridge suffers from some kind of phobia. It's quite a common one. As far as I'm aware, most snakes just want to get as far away from us as possible. I think we can call it a night. I'll see you bright and early tomorrow."

"Good night, boss," Smith said and walked towards his car. He turned around and walked back. "Something doesn't make any sense."

"What doesn't?"

"Matt McLean kept an up-to-date stock of anti-venom in a fridge in the basement, as well as a selection of syringes. Why didn't he inject himself with it? He had anti-venoms for all the poisonous snakes."

"We'll cover all of this tomorrow," Brownhill said. "Actually today – it's almost two in the morning. Go home and get some sleep."

Smith knew he wasn't going to be able to get any sleep. He made some coffee and took it through to the living room. Whitton had obviously gone up to bed and the dogs must have joined her. Smith's mind was racing. He knew he was going to be dog-tired at work in a few hours time, but he needed to process everything while it was still bouncing around in his head.

"What do we know?" he said out loud. "We know Matt McLean kept snakes in his basement. We also know he had a supply of anti-venoms."

Matt had told him the snakes he had right now were not particularly dangerous.

Apart from the Death Adder.

Smith switched on his computer, waited for it to boot up and typed *Death Adder* in the search bar. The results made for disturbing reading. The Common Death Adder is only found in Australia where it is the snake with the longest fangs. Untreated, its bites have a 50-60% mortality rate, and it is the fastest-striking venomous snake in the world. One piece of information about the snake caught Smith's eye. In the article it was claimed that the Death Adder is a rather reluctant biter, and will rarely bite unless severely provoked.

"We need to find out if Matt McLean was bitten or injected," Smith said in a voice no more than a whisper.

Smith finished the coffee and went outside for a smoke. It was bitterly cold now and there were no clouds in the sky. He breathed in the crisp early-morning December air and tried to clear his head of all unimportant facts. Something was nagging away at him – something vital, but each time he came close to realising what it was it slipped away from him again. He wasn't going to get any closer right now – he needed to sleep, and although he knew he wouldn't sleep a wink, he went back inside the house and made his way up to bed.

CHAPTER FORTY ONE

It was not yet nine in the morning, but the switchboard at York police station had already received over a hundred phone calls from people claiming to have received suspicious packages in the post that morning. After dealing with prank-calls, time-wasters and general whackos all night the team who had been assigned to the switchboard breathed a collective sigh of relief when their shift was over. Now the morning shift could take over the flood of panic-stricken residents who would no doubt call in asking the police to check that their copy of the latest *Reader's Digest* was not in fact a lethal venom-infected letter.

Tony Wood had also worked a long night shift. It was the fifth twelve-hour shift he'd worked in as many days. The eight-til-eight was not a shift everyone would relish but it suited Tony down to the ground. Not only did the antisocial hours pay well, but the tasks Tony Wood had to perform during the night as the night watchman at the football stadium were minimal and they afforded him ample time to indulge in his only passion – poetry. Whether it be reading, writing or listening to it on an Audio Book, poetry was Tony's life. He was fifty-five years old, he'd never been married, but he'd always had poetry. Tony prided himself on two things, and he made a point of telling anybody unfortunate enough to have to listen what these two things were. Tony never read the newspapers, and he never watched television. So it was the two things Tony most prided himself on that meant, when the day's post landed on the mat by the front door with a quiet thud – coupled with the fact that he'd just worked five twelve hour night shifts, and was oblivious to what had been going on in the outside world, that was about to cost him his life.

* * *

Smith sat back on the chair in his office and stretched his arms behind his head. Considering he'd had roughly two hours sleep he felt surprisingly alert. He knew today was going to be a taxing one – there was already a commotion by the front desk when he walked in, but he'd walked straight through it and headed for the solace of his office. There had been no reports of any envenomations yet, and his phoned hadn't rung with the ominous – *I want to live.*

Yang Chu came into the office. The young DC looked exhausted. He sat down opposite Smith and yawned.

"It's chaos down there," he said. "People have brought in packages and dumped them in front of the front desk. I don't know how we're going to find the time to sift through that lot. This nutter certainly picked a fine time to do this what with the Christmas postal rush already in full swing."

"Somebody else can deal with it," Smith told him. "The DI has called a briefing for half-nine. And I'd quite like a bit of peace and quiet before then." Yang Chu yawned again and stood up. "Hint taken, Sarge. I'll see you at the briefing then."

When Smith walked into the small conference room and saw that Superintendent Jeremy Smyth was in attendance he knew straight away which direction the briefing was heading. Whenever Smyth gate-crashed their meetings it invariably meant one thing and one thing only. Public relations.

As the rest of the team gathered Smith smiled inwardly when he realised the expressions on their faces upon seeing Smyth, mirrored his own. They were bogged down as it was and the last thing they needed at this stage of an investigation was the input of bungling public-school berk, Smyth.

Smith was relieved when Chalmers walked in. If there was anybody who could steer the Super in the right direction it was the DCI. He sat down next to Smith.

"Have you been popping pills?" Chalmers asked.

"Of course not. Why do you ask?"

"Because you look more awake than any of the rest of them. Look at them – like a bunch of zombies."

"It's been a rough week, boss. Probably the roughest any of us have ever had. And it looks like it's going to get much worse."

He nodded towards the Superintendent who was gawping at something on his mobile phone with his mouth wide open.

"Don't worry about old Smyth," Chalmers said. "If he starts his irrelevant crap, I'll sort him out."

"Thanks, boss. We don't need this right now."

"Let's make a start," Brownhill said. "Before we begin, Superintendent Smyth would like to say a few words."

"Good morning, everyone," Smyth remained seated which was most unusual. "I understand that this week has been particularly draining for all of you. Three murders in the space of a few days."

"Four, sir, "Chalmers corrected him. "There was another one last night."

"Oh my," Smyth looked like a schoolgirl whose pet rabbit had just died.

"Four then. It truly is a terrible business, but I have every confidence in the team sitting here before me. You may feel right now that all hope is lost but dig deep. I know you can find it within yourselves to overcome the fatigue you are feeling right now and bring this matter to its rightful conclusion. My crime statistics run up to the end of this month, so let's crack this one before then. What do you say? Are we going to sit back and let this beat us? Or are we going to step up? Find that extra gear and show the general public what the York Police are made of? What do you say?"

"We'll do what we can, sir." It was Chalmers. "Thanks for the pep-talk, but we really must crack on with the briefing."

"Very well," Superintendent Smyth got up, nodded to Chalmers and left the room.

Everyone in the small conference room sat in silence for a few moments after Smyth had gone.

Bridge broke the silence. He stood up, and spoke in a voice that mimicked Smyth's perfectly.

"We shall fight them on the beaches."

Yang Chu and Whitton started to giggle.

"We shall never surrender," Bridge added, this time in a much louder voice. He raised his hand in the air at the same time.

The whole room erupted.

"That's enough," Brownhill said, although even she had a grin on her face she couldn't hide. "Let's get started, shall we? Smith?"

"We've got something to go on," Smith began. "A name. Just before Matthew McLean died he whispered a name in my ear. Boris Boronov. We have to assume this is the same BB the journalist from the York Gazette referred to. And…" Smith wasn't exactly sure how he was going to phrase his next sentence. "And I think I've come up with a motive."

He looked around the room. All eyes were glued to him.

"Boronov," he said. "Is not a common name. I'm sure you all remember Viktor Boronov."

"He's the bastard who tried to kill you," Bridge said.

"More than once," Smith added. "But now he's dead."

"And you think there's another Boronov out there who is carrying on where he left off?" Brownhill asked.

"It's the only explanation. And that's what we need to concentrate all our efforts on. We need to find this Boris Boronov."

"We've got something else," Brownhill said. "Grant pulled an all-nighter and we've got fingerprints. There were prints on Matthew McLean's telephone that were not Mr McLean's. Therefore, we can assume they belong to our venom killer. The same prints were found on fragments of glass from the snake container. Unfortunately, they are not on our data base but we've got our first piece of real evidence. And I believe the very fact that Mr McLean was killed leads us to assume he knew something about the killer that would possibly lead us to him. We need to find out what that is."

"The glass containers were all labelled," Smith said. "Did Webber check the one that was smashed?"

"Of course," Brownhill opened up a folder in front of her. "Acanthophis Antarcticus. Better known as the Death Adder. The basement has been searched thoroughly – the snake was nowhere to be seen, so it's safe to assume the killer took it with him."

"Matt's business was exotic snakes," Smith said. "That's a very specialist industry. I would think that everybody in that industry knows everybody else."

"That's what we need to concentrate on."

"What about Dr Marx?" Yang Chu said. "She's a snake woman. She must know the main players in the business."

"Where is she?" Whitton asked. "I thought she was supposed to be helping us in the investigation."

"Unfortunately Dr Marx isn't contracted to the York police," Brownhill said. "She has her own obligations, and she is merely helping out in an advisory capacity."

"Yang Chu's right," Smith said. "If anybody knows anything about Boris Boronov or BB as he calls himself, it's Dr Lillian Marx."

CHAPTER FORTY TWO

Smith didn't need to show his ID to the long-haired man at the front desk of the Clifton snake centre this time – he merely shrugged and nodded in the direction of the milking lab. Smith walked down the long corridor and was about to open the door at the end when he heard raised voices coming from inside the room. A heated argument was clearly in progress. Smith couldn't make out the words, but he could hear that a disagreement was taking place. He knocked on the door and the argument stopped. A few seconds later, the door opened, and a very red-faced Dr Lillian Marx stood there with a scowl on her face.

"Is this a bad time?" Smith asked her.

He looked inside the room. The same, short black-haired man was standing by one of the snake cages. He was trying to look busy but he wasn't doing a very good job of it. He was clearly agitated about something.

"What do you want?" Dr Marx said.

"A word," Smith said. "I'm suddenly starving. Do they do breakfast in this place?"

Dr Marx's face softened slightly. "I'm finished here for the day. I know a place just round the corner. They do the best bacon and egg roll in York."

* * *

Smith wiped the crumbs from the corner of his mouth and took a sip of coffee. Dr Marx hadn't been lying about the bacon and egg roll at The Lion Coffee House.

"I couldn't help overhearing back there," he said. "What were you two arguing about?"

"It was nothing," Dr Marx said. "Greg and I get a bit over-passionate about things sometimes."

"Greg?"

"He's one of the volunteers at the centre. He's very dedicated and he's got a kind heart, but we tend to disagree a lot. Anyway, what was it you wanted to talk to me about?"

"The snake business," Smith said. "It must be a close-knit industry."

"I suppose so."

"So, you know most of the people in that industry? You knew Matt McLean."

"I heard what happened. It must have been awful. The Death Adder bite is a nasty one."

"Does the name Boris Boronov mean anything to you?" Smith came straight out with it.

"No," Dr Marx replied immediately.

"Are you sure? Boris Boronov? What about BB?"

"Never heard of him. Who is he?"

"We believe he's the man responsible for the recent envenomations. He could be using a false name. This man has access to snake venom, and he knows what venom to use. Therefore I think he's somebody in your field of vision."

"What exactly are you implying?"

"I'm not implying anything," Smith said. "Let me put it another way. If I wanted to kill someone with the poison from a snake, how would I do it?"

"That's a ridiculous question."

"No it's not. How would I kill somebody with snake venom? Where would I get hold of the venom?"

"I told you before. You could only get that sort of thing illegally. On the black market."

"Where?" Smith demanded and banged his fist on the table.

An elderly couple on the table next to them stared at him with wide eyes.

"I have to get to the hospital," Dr Marx was clearly annoyed. "And I don't appreciate being spoken to like this. I volunteered my help and you're treating me like a suspect."

Smith's mobile phone started to ring in his pocket. Dr Marx stood up to leave. Smith took out the phone, saw it was a number he didn't recognise and rejected the call.

"I'm sorry," he said as his phone rang again.

"I have to go," Dr Marx insisted.

Smith pressed *reject call* once more. "I'll give you a lift. I need to speak to Kenny Bean about something anyway. I'm sorry – this investigation is really starting to get to me. Can we start again?"

His phone beeped to tell him he'd received a voice message.

"How did you get into snakes in the first place?" Smith asked.

Dr Marx had accepted his offer of a lift to the hospital.

"I've always been fascinated by them," she replied. "I wanted to become a herpetologist, but my father insisted I follow in his footsteps and study medicine. So, I obliged, but then I rebelled. After medical school, I did a stint in pathology, and then I travelled overseas and got into volunteer work researching anti-venoms."

"Sounds interesting," Smith said. "And terrifying."

"That's just the thing. Education is everything. People have this unfounded fear of snakes."

"I'm more of a dog person," Smith said. "At least if a dog nips you, you don't have to worry about pegging it."

"A snake will not bite you unless it feels threatened. Almost all snake bites are the result of people encroaching on territory that has belonged to the snake long before people arrived. A snake does what it does to protect itself, and I like that. It's nature at its purest."

"If you say so. I'll take my chances with a dog."

They walked inside the hospital together.

"I have to get changed," Dr Marx said. "Thanks for the lift."

"No problem," Smith said. "And I'm sorry again about earlier."

"I've forgotten about it already."

Dr Kenny Bean was in his office tapping frantically on his laptop. His door was open so Smith walked straight in.

"Kenny," he said. "I hope I'm not interrupting anything important."

"Reports," Kenny said without turning round. "If there's one thing about this job that riles me it's reports. What can I do for you?"

He stopped typing and looked at Smith.

"Did you manage to have a look at the man who was brought in last night?" Smith asked him. "Matthew McLean?"

"He's dead," Dr Bean said with a deadpan face. "Without a shadow of a doubt."

"Please, Kenny. I'm not in the mood."

"Killjoy. We examined him first thing. Nasty business."

"The wound on his neck," Smith said. "Was that caused by a snake bite?"

"Definitely. The incisions made by the fangs were clear. The poor bastard got a dose of neurotoxic venom straight into the carotid artery. The poison was diverted from his heart but it was delivered first-class throughout his body. He didn't stand a chance."

"So it was definitely a bite and not an injection of venom?"

"Didn't you hear what I just said?"

"Sorry," Smith said. "I just wanted to be a hundred percent certain."

"Will that be all?" Dr Bean asked. "I'm longing to finish this report."

CHAPTER FORTY THREE

Smith reached inside his pocket to take out his car keys, his key ring hooked on his mobile phone and it fell onto the tarmac next to his car. He picked it up and checked to see if it was still working. The screen was intact. There was a light flashing to tell him he had a voice message. He opened up his voicemail, listened to the recorded message and waited for the voice message. He froze when he heard the man's high-pitched voice.

'I want to live'

"Fuck."

Smith brought up the number of the last call, and with shaky hands wrote it down on a notepad he kept in the glove compartment. He phoned the switchboard at the station.

PC Baldwin answered straight away.

"Baldwin," Smith said. "I need a phone number traced immediately. It's a landline number. I need a name and address. This is urgent."

He gave her the number and rang off.

The next three minutes seemed more like three days, and when the screen on Smith's mobile phone displayed the number of the switchboard at the station his fingers fumbled on the screen to hit the *answer* icon.

"Smith," he said eventually.

"Sir," it was Baldwin. "The number is registered to an Anthony Wood. His address is 67 Reeve Street."

"Thanks, Baldwin. I need an ambulance there ten minutes ago, and round up the team. Tell them I'll meet them there."

Smith started the car and drove out of the hospital car park with a screech of brakes. Reeve Street was just around the corner from his own house. This was now getting far too close to home for his liking. The speedometer on the dashboard read 90 miles per hour. Smith slowed down but still took the corner too quickly and ended up on the opposite side of the road, narrowly missing a bus. The elderly driver looked on with wide eyes as Smith swerved back onto the other side of the road. He turned into Reeve Street and stopped outside number 67. The ambulance and the rest of the team hadn't arrived yet.

Smith ran up the driveway and tried the door handle. The door was locked. He aimed a kick where he reckoned the lock to be but the door didn't budge. He kicked again and felt something give. His foot was in agony. The door still wouldn't open. He ignored the pain in his foot and kicked with all the strength he could muster. Sirens could be heard in the distance. The wood on the door splintered and it opened with a crunch. Smith hobbled inside.

He found Anthony Wood in the hallway. There was a cordless telephone lying on the carpet next to him. Smith didn't need to check for a pulse to see that he was dead. His eyes were open and his tongue was sticking out of his wide-open mouth. The skin on his face had tightened and his eyelids appeared to have stretched. The sirens came nearer until they were directly outside the house. The ambulance was too late.

Smith sat on the carpet with his back against the wall. Whitton and Brownhill arrived and came inside. Two paramedics came in behind them. Bridge and Yang Chu brought up the rear.

"I was too late," Smith said. "I should have answered my fucking phone. He's dead because I ignored his call."

Whitton walked over to him and placed a hand on his shoulder but Smith shrugged it off.

"He's dead because of me," he said.

He got to his feet and limped out of the house. He got into his car and sped off down the street.

"Maybe I should go after him," Whitton suggested.

"You'll never catch him," Brownhill said. "He just needs to let off a bit of steam. He'll be fine."

Grant Webber walked up to them. He glanced down at the lifeless body of Anthony Wood.

"Bloody hell."

"His name's Anthony Wood," Brownhill told him. "Fifty-five years old. He phoned Smith, but it seems Smith got here too late."

"What's wrong with Smith?" Webber asked. "He drove off like a maniac."

"He's blaming himself," Whitton said. "He thinks it's his fault."

"Did you find the note?" Webber said.

"We've only just got here."

Webber found it in the living room. He donned a pair of gloves, picked it up and read it. It was the same as the others. Hand written in black capital letters.

'CONGRATULATIONS. YOU HAVE BEEN CHOSEN TO RECEIVE A SPECIAL PRIZE – A GIFT FROM A BUNGARUS CAERULEUS. YOUR REWARD IS OBLIVION. SHOULD YOU DECIDE NOT TO ACCEPT THIS PRIZE, PHONE THE NUMBER BELOW AND REPEAT THESE FOUR SIMPLE WORDS – I WANT TO LIVE.'

Smith's mobile phone number was written at the bottom again.

"Bungarus Caeruleus," Webber read. "What the hell is that?"

Whitton opened up Google on her phone. "It's a Common Krait. Incredibly dangerous. Untreated mortality rate of 80%."

"Krait?" Yang Chu repeated. "That's the name of the snake the bloke who phoned in yesterday mentioned. The one who phoned from Matthew McLean's phone. He said there was no anti-venom for it."

"I have to get hold of Smith," Whitton said. "I have to tell him there was nothing he could have done."

She went outside and took out her phone. She dialled Smith's number but it went straight to voicemail.

"The venom that killed Anthony Wood," she said after the recorded message. "Was from a Krait. There is no anti-venom for that particular snake. There was nothing we could have done for him. I'm worried about you. Call me as soon as you get this."

She hung up and went back inside the house.

Grant Webber was holding something in his hand. It was the same metal contraption they'd found at the other envenomation scenes. He sighed and placed it inside a plastic evidence bag.

"It's not like we're going to get anything from it," he said to Brownhill. "And this crime scene is going to turn out just like the rest. A non-crime scene."

"Give it the once-over anyway," Brownhill said. "We might get lucky."

* * *

Smith parked outside his house and slammed his fists on the steering wheel. He felt like a drink. People were dying because of him. The more he thought about it the more he came to the conclusion that people were always dying because of him. He made a mental list of all the people he'd known who had met an untimely end due to something he'd done or somebody he'd annoyed. The list was disturbingly long. Too long. He really felt like a drink, but he knew it would only end badly. He decided on a better plan of action. He got out of the car and went inside his house.

CHAPTER FORTY FOUR

Theakston and Fred were racing towards the lake at the bottom of the park. Theakston was finding it hard to keep up with the repugnant Pug. Fred was much slimmer and fitter than the lazy Bull Terrier. Smith walked quickly after them. He hadn't taken the dogs to the park for a very long time. There wasn't a puff of breeze in the air but it was bitterly cold. Smith caught up with the dogs and sat down on the bench overlooking the lake. There was a thin layer of ice on the surface of the water and the dogs were taking a keen interest in it. Theakston bounded off around the lake, probably wondering where the ducks had gone. Fred was too busy studying his repulsive face in the mirror of the lake to notice.

Smith took out his phone and saw he had a missed call from Whitton. He knew his outburst earlier was totally uncalled for but he didn't feel like discussing it so he put his phone back in his pocket. He tried to put together the pieces of everything that had happened since the beginning of the week. When did it all start?

Was it when the first victim received their *prize* or was it long before that? *Boris Boronov*? Smith thought.

Just hearing that surname in his head made him shiver. It couldn't just be a coincidence. It had to have something to do with the man Whitton had fatally stabbed earlier in the year.

Theakston and Fred checked in and then both dogs headed off to the side of the lake they hadn't yet explored. Smith tried to go over the sequence of events once more. The victims were irrelevant – he'd realised that pretty much from the start. They were all just unfortunate pawns in a sick-minded individual's chess game. That part was clear. The way they were killed still baffled Smith. Why snake venom? Smith had to admit these killings were as close as he'd ever come to seeing a perfect murder. There was nothing to link the victims to the murderer – the scenes of the murders revealed no evidence because the killer wasn't present at the time the murders were carried out, and the murder weapons themselves revealed nothing about the killer other than the fact that he was extremely adept with his hands.

"What do we know about the murderer?" Smith spoke out loud. Going through everything in his head wasn't helping. Maybe it would be easier to hold a conversation with himself.

"We know he's a man with a lisp," he continued. "And we know he has access to snake venom. Particularly potent snake venom. We know now that he was acquainted with Matt McLean. There was no indication of forced entry into Matt's house therefore Matt must have let him in. Why? Why did Matt McLean invite this man into his house?"

Theakston and Fred reappeared. Both of them had slowed down considerably – they were both desperately unfit. The two dogs dropped to the ground at Smith's feet.

"Come on, you two," Smith said to them. "Help me out with this. Who is this maniac, and what does he want with me?"

Theakston and Fred ignored him. They were more interested in seeing who could pant the louder.

Smith thought of something. It was something Phil Davies from the York Gazette had said. Somebody claiming to be the killer had phoned him and told him there would be another one – a particularly quick one, and then there would be one more. And then it would stop.

"Why is he going to stop?" Smith asked nobody in particular. "Why not keep on taunting me?"

Then it dawned on him. It dawned on him with terrifying certainty.

"He's going to stop because the last one is going to be personal."

* * *

Smith arrived at the station twenty minutes later. He'd run up the path in the park followed by two dumbfounded dogs – he'd let them in the house, and driven straight to the station. He headed straight for Brownhill's office.

"Are you back with us then?" the DI asked before Smith had even got through the door.

"I think I've figured something out," Smith told her.

"Go on."

"This latest one was the penultimate one. The killer phoned the Gazette. He said there will be another one – a particularly quick one, there will be one more and then it will stop. He's going to come after me or someone close to me. Where's Whitton?"

"She, Bridge and Yang Chu are doing some research."

"Research?" Smith said.

"Research into snakes."

"How's that going to help?"

"It can't hurt. Smith, this latest killing."

"Yes?"

"There was nothing you could have done about it. The man was injected with the venom from a Krait. Even if he'd gone to hospital immediately, he would have died anyway. That's what the killer meant about it being a particularly quick one."

"Is Matt McLean's house still taped up?" Smith asked.

"I believe so. The snakes still haven't been removed."

"I'm going over there. There's something I need to check."

"What's that?"

"I'll let you know when I've figured it out."

Smith was halfway out the door.

"Smith," Brownhill said.

He turned around.

"Phone your wife," the DI said. "She's worried about you. And that's an order."

"Yes, boss," Smith said and left the room.

CHAPTER FORTY FIVE

Smith stepped under the police tape preventing access to Matt McLean's house. He'd obtained the key and he inserted it in the keyhole. He opened the door and went inside. He wasn't quite sure what he was looking for, but there had to be something inside the house that could shed some light on how Matt was acquainted with the venom murderer.

There has to be something here, he thought.

He went inside the living room. There was hardly any furniture and there were no ornaments or pictures on the wall. It occurred to Smith that Matt hadn't been living here very long. He walked up to the small sideboard that stood against the far wall. It consisted of two drawers and a small cupboard. Smith opened the cupboard. There was nothing inside except two books about poisonous snakes. He tried one of the drawers. It was locked. The second one was also locked. Smith walked through to the kitchen to see if he could find something to open the drawers. He found a suitable knife and took it with him to the living room. After a bit of effort he managed to get the first drawer open. Inside there were a few opened letters and a paperweight shaped like a cobra with its hood spread.

Smith found what he was looking for in the second drawer. It was a black address book – the kind you rarely saw anymore with the advent of mobile phones and tablets. Smith opened it up and scanned through the pages. His own mobile number was in there as was his address.

How did Matt know my address? he thought. *And why does he have my address in this book?*

Boris Boronov wasn't in the book. Smith checked again with the same results.

"Damn it," he said and put the address book in his pocket.

He left the room and headed for the staircase that led down to the basement. He opened the metal door and went inside. The heaters were still on and the room was oppressively hot. The remains of the smashed glass container were still lying on the floor. None of the snakes in the other containers appeared to be moving.

What kind of pets do these things make? Smith thought as he looked at the cold-blooded creatures lying dormant inside the cages.

There was fingerprint powder everywhere. Grant Webber had obviously done a very thorough job.

Smith realised he was wasting his time down in the basement. Besides the containers and their slithery occupants, there was nothing else in the room except the small fridge containing the anti-venom. Smith opened it up and looked inside. The vials were neatly lined up on the top shelf. Beneath them lay syringes of various sizes. Smith looked at the vials of anti-venom again.

There was one missing.

There was a clear gap in the row of vials.

Smith heard a noise from upstairs and he jumped. It was the sound of a telephone ringing. He made his way up the stairs and picked up the receiver.

"You won't find anything there, Detective Smith." The man spoke with a lisp.

"What the hell do you want?" Smith knew straight away who it was.

"Do you know what a Taipan is?"

"What is it you want?"

"It will kill a fully grown man in less than an hour." The man ignored Smith's question. "So, you can just imagine what it will do to a child who's not yet turned two."

Smith's stomach felt suddenly warm. He felt like he was going to be sick.

"I'm coming for you," he said but the line had already gone dead.

Smith sank down onto the carpet and sat with his back to the wall. He felt exhausted and absolutely powerless. How was he supposed to stop a man who had killed people without even being there? He had no idea where this monster was, and he still didn't know why he was doing this. Smith took out his phone and dialled Whitton's number. It went straight to voicemail.

"Whitton," Smith said. "Phone me as soon as you get this. This is extremely important. I love you."

He didn't know what to do. He took some consolation in the fact that Laura was staying with Whitton's parents. The murderer couldn't possibly know that.

How did he know I was here in Matt McLean's house? The thought hit him like an arrow in the gut.

He got off the floor and ran outside. He looked up and down the street – there were a few cars parked on either side of the road, but they all appeared to be empty. His thoughts wandered back to when he was followed by the black hatchback.

Has this maniac been watching me the whole time?

His phone started to ring in his pocket. It was Whitton.

"Where have you been?" Smith said.

"Where have *you* been? I've been worried sick about you."

"I'm at Matt McLean's house," Smith told her. "I thought I might find something here to explain how Matt knew this Boris Boronov lunatic. There's nothing here. I think you or Laura might be in danger. I want you to stay with your parents until all this is over."

"What about you?"

"He's not going to kill me, Whitton. I don't think he wants me dead. I think he wants me to suffer. Will you do that? Just until he's caught."

"OK," Whitton agreed. "My mum has asked if we want to go there this evening anyway. She's going to cook us her special roast."

"Sounds good. Where are you now?"

"Taking a break. We didn't find much on the net. There's only one snake facility in York, and the traders in exotic reptiles don't appear to advertise much online."

"I'm going to catch this bastard, Whitton," Smith said. "I promise you. I'll see you back at the station. I'm on my way now."

Smith opened his car door and got inside. He started the engine and drove away from Matt Mclean's house. He didn't notice the black hatchback parked in a driveway a few doors down on the opposite side of the road. It pulled out and drove off in the opposite direction to the way Smith had driven.

CHAPTER FORTY SIX

Whitton was in the car park talking to DCI Chalmers when Smith arrived. He got out of the car, rushed up to her and flung his arms around her.

"Bloody newlyweds," Chalmers said. "Give it a few years and you'll be greeting each other with a polite nod of the head."

"Are you alright?" Whitton asked.

"Not really," Smith admitted. "Have I missed anything?"

"Nothing. We're banging our heads against one brick wall after the other. The DI has told us to call it a day. We're not getting anywhere at the moment."

"Don't go home," Smith said. "It's not safe. Go straight to your parents' house. I'll see you there in about an hour."

"Where are you going?"

"I need to feed the dogs," Smith told her. "Then I need to speak to Dr Lillian Marx about something. Do you want me to pick anything up for you from home?"

"Just a change of clothes," Whitton said. "And my toothbrush."

"What's going on?" Chalmers said.

Smith told him about the phone call from the venom murderer.

"I'll follow you home," the DCI told Whitton when Smith had finished. "Just to be safe." He turned to Smith. "What about you? If what you've said is true he could be waiting for you somewhere."

"He won't be," Smith was certain.

He hugged Whitton again. "I'll see you in an hour or so."

Smith drove away from the police station. He turned on the hands-free and told his phone to call Dr Kenny Bean.

"Detective," Kenny answered. "What have you got to annoy me with now?"

"Kenny, is Dr Marx there with you?"

"She left about an hour ago. She said she had some work to do at the Clifton Snake Centre."

"What do they actually do there at the Centre?" Smith asked.

"All sorts. Research, rehabilitation, that kind of thing. I'm not overly fond of snakes myself, but I suppose it takes all sorts."

"Thanks, Kenny," Smith said and rang off.

* * *

The man with the long hair was speaking on the phone when Smith walked into the Clifton snake centre. Smith waited for him to finish the call.

"Dr Marx is in the office," the man told him. "Is she expecting you?"

"Do I need to make an appointment?"

"No," the man smiled. "I just thought it was something a receptionist ought to say. It's the second door on the right."

"Thanks," Smith said and walked down the corridor.

The second door on the right was closed. Smith could hear voices inside. One of them he recognised as being Dr Marx's, but the other one was unfamiliar. He knocked on the door and the voices stopped.

The door was opened by Dr Marx. She seemed surprised to see him.

"Can I help you?" she asked.

"I need to ask you something," Smith said.

"Come in. We've finished here, anyway."

Smith went inside. The same short man who was there earlier was sitting behind a small desk.

"Afternoon," Smith said to him.

He nodded in reply but did not make eye contact.

"Greg," Dr Marx said to him. "Would you mind if DS Smith and I spoke in private?"

"That's not necessary," Smith said. "Maybe he can help too. I need to ask about anti-venom."

The man called Greg stood up and left the room without uttering a word.

"He's very shy," Dr Marx explained. "Take a seat. What was that about anti-venom?"

Smith sat down. "The Taipan. Where can I get anti-venom for a Taipan?"

"Inland or Coastal?" Dr Marx asked.

"Excuse me?"

"There are two very different species. The Coastal Taipan is very aggressive, but its venom is less potent than its cousin, the Inland Taipan."

"Aren't the anti-venoms the same?"

"They are, but the dosage will depend on the species."

"Do you have any anti-venom for a Taipan?" Smith asked.

"Not at hand. Why do you ask?"

"Because I believe there is a great risk of someone being injected with Taipan poison very soon and I want to be prepared."

"I'll see what I can do. Will there be anything else?"

Smith looked at the clock on the wall. "That's all, thank you. I'm late for a roast meal at the in-laws."

"Sounds lovely."

"Whitton and Laura are going to be staying there until all this is over."

"I see," Dr Marx said. "I suppose it's for the best."

Smith stood up. "Thanks again for all your help."

CHAPTER FORTY SEVEN

Smith wasn't hungry as he stood outside the terraced house that Whitton's parents called home – the events over the past week had dampened his appetite, but when Whitton's father, Harold opened the door and the aroma of roast beef wafted outside, Smith was suddenly starving.

"You don't have to knock, lad," Harold told him. "How many times do I have to tell you that?"

"Good evening, Mr Whitton," Smith said and stepped inside. "It just doesn't feel right walking straight in."

"Get used to it. And it's Harold. Mr Whitton makes me feel old. Beer?"

"That sounds great."

Smith went into the kitchen. Whitton was standing next to her mother, Jane by the sink. Smith walked up and kissed his wife on the top of the head.

"Something smells delicious. Good evening, Mrs Whitton."

"Hello, love," Jane turned and looked at him. "You look tired."

Harold appeared with a beer and handed it to Smith.

"Thanks," Smith took a long drink. "It's been a long week. Where's Laura?"

"Upstairs asleep," Jane told him. "She'll be about ready for a feed."

"Thanks for having her," Smith said.

"She's been a little angel. Erica was a bit of a terror at that age."

"Thanks, Mum," Whitton said.

"She hasn't changed much," Smith added.

"Food'll be about half an hour," Jane informed him. "I hope you're hungry."

"I'll stick some tunes on," Harold said and walked out of the room.

"Not Val Doonican though," his wife shouted after him. "We've got young un's in the house."

"I'll help him choose," Smith offered.

Smith and Harold had compromised, and now The Shadows were playing. Hank Marvin's tinny guitar had started to play the opening bars of Apache.

"Terrible business about these venom murders," Harold said. "Do you have any leads?"

"We're working on it," Smith didn't really feel like talking about the investigation.

"Something will jump out at you, lad," Harold said. "Don't try and force it." Smith realised it was the first time Smith had ever discussed work with Whitton's Dad. Harold Whitton had been a teacher in one of the local secondary schools. He'd been retired for a few years now, but his mind was still incredibly sharp.

"That's the best piece of advice I've heard in a long time," Smith said to him.

"It's true. I've done the Guardian cryptic crossword for nigh on thirty years every morning. And I've cracked every one of them. When I'm stuck on a clue, I don't over-think it. That's a total waste of time. I leave it, and more often than not, when I come back to it, it's so bloody simple I don't understand what stumped me in the first place."

"Harold," Jane had come in the room. "Language."

Harold looked at Smith. "Did I swear?"

Smith laughed. "I didn't hear anything."

"Can I get you a refill?" Harold asked him.

"Just what the doctor ordered."

The roast beef was delicious. Smith and Whitton decided they would wait until after the meal before bringing up the matter of Whitton staying with them.

"I need to ask you a favour," Whitton said.

"Sounds serious," Harold said.

"Would it be alright if I stayed here for a few days?"

"Of course, it's alright, love," Harold said. "You don't need to ask. There's nowt wrong is there?"

He addressed the question to Smith.

"It's just a precaution," Smith told him. "We're probably worrying about nothing."

"Is there something we ought to know?" Harold asked. "Is my daughter in any danger?"

"I don't know," was all Smith could think of to say. "I just think it's best that she stays here until this venom thing is all over."

"Right then," Jane said. "Who's for some pudding? I've made a Jam Roly Poly."

Smith breathed out a sigh of relief. "Sounds delicious."

When the meal was finished, Smith offered to wash the dishes.

"You'll do no such thing," Jane said. "You boys go and relax in the lounge. Erica and me can sort out the dishes."

Smith took his beer through to the lounge and sat next to Harold on the three-seater sofa.

"Right, lad," his father-in-law said. "I want to know what's going on."

Smith told him everything. He told him how the venom nightmare had all started and about how it was somehow connected to him. Harold Whitton finished the rest of the beer and looked Smith directly in the eye.

"She'll be safe here," he said after a few seconds. "But I want you to promise me one thing."

"Of course."

"Catch him. Catch this maniac and nail his balls to the wall."

"Harold!" Jane's timing was perfect as usual. "What kind of way is that to talk?"

Harold nodded to Smith and they both smiled.

"I'll see you at work tomorrow," Smith said to Whitton on the doorstep.

"My mum said you're welcome to stay here as well," Whitton told him.

"I'll be fine at home. I don't want to leave the dogs on their own."

He hugged her tightly and walked to his car.

CHAPTER FORTY EIGHT

Smith unlocked his door, went inside and locked the door behind him. The house was in darkness and it was freezing inside. He'd forgotten to set the timer on the central heating. He switched on the light in the hallway and turned on the heating. Theakston and Fred appeared from the living room and started circling him, their tails wagging madly. They could smell the contents of the plastic bag that Smith held in his hand, and it was obviously driving them mad. Whitton's mother had given Smith the leftover beef and the bone from the joint to take home for the dogs.

Smith took the leftovers to the kitchen, divided them in two and emptied them into the dogs' bowls. The bowls were empty in thirty seconds and both dogs were now staring up at Smith, begging for more.

"I've never seen such pigs," Smith said.

He filled up the bowls with dog food but after the beef, dog food just wouldn't do.

"That's all there is," Smith told them.

He boiled the kettle and made some coffee. The clock on the microwave told him it was nine-thirty. Smith wasn't at all tired. He took the coffee through to the living room and put on some music. The first track of Joe Bonamassa's *Blues of Desperation* oozed out of the speakers. The meal at Whitton's parents' house had been just what the doctor ordered – Smith had always liked his in-laws, and he had the utmost respect for Harold. Whitton's Dad had taken the news about the threat posed by the venom killer like a true Yorkshireman. Stoically. Smith could now see where Whitton got her philosophy in life from. Smith often wondered he could be more like her, but he knew it was far too late to change now.

The opening riff of *No Good Place for the Lonely* came on and Smith smiled. There was something about Blues that lifted his spirits. He finished his coffee and went outside for a cigarette. The sky was clear once more and the air was crisp. It was going to be yet another freezing-cold day tomorrow. He sat on the bench and thought about what Whitton's Dad had said to him. *Don't try and force it.*

He was right. Smith had lost count of how many times he'd been at his wits end during an investigation and the answer had jumped out at him when he least expected it. It was sound advice.

He went back inside. Joe Bonamassa was singing about what he'd known for a very long time. The house was much warmer now.

What do we know?

Smith asked himself the question he'd asked himself over and over.

What do we know?

They knew virtually nothing. The only clear part of the picture was an inkling of a motive. And Smith had something to do with that. They also had a name.

Boris Boronov. How did he come into the equation?

Smith turned on his PC. He made another cup of coffee while he waited for it to boot up. He sat down at typed in Viktor Boronov in the search bar. The first page that appeared listed various newspaper articles and online reports pertaining to the illegal human organ trafficking ring that Viktor Boronov had been instrumental. Smith clicked on one of them and flinched when he found himself staring at his own face on the screen. There was also a photograph of Viktor Boronov at the bottom. Smith had actually forgotten what he looked like. The sinister eyes seemed to bore a hole straight through you. Smith closed his eyes. He could still see the face in his mind. And that's when it dawned on him. He'd seen that face recently. He was certain of it. He'd seen Viktor Boronov's face. Or at least some version of it.

He carried on scrolling down until he found something that caught his eye. Very little was known about Viktor Boronov aside from what the press had managed to dig up from previous reports. Smith actually knew more information about the man than any of the articles could provide him with. He had a sister, Nadia who was killed as she was about to shoot Smith. He was born in the former Soviet Union and grew up in what was now Estonia. He had a hand in more than his far share of organised crime activities before he was killed. There was nothing on the screen that Smith didn't already know.

He switched off the computer and went outside for a last cigarette of the day. When he came back in, he made sure the door was locked. He rounded up the dogs and went upstairs. He didn't think he was going to be able to sleep, but he drifted off almost as soon as he'd closed his eyes.

CHAPTER FORTY NINE

Smith woke to the sound of two dogs snoring in stereo. Theakston's grunt was more low-pitched than the grotesque Pug's snort. The noise they made together made Smith smile. He got out of bed, dressed and went downstairs to make coffee. There was a letter lying on the mat by the front door. It was too early for the first post of the day, and Smith was instantly on his guard. He got a long knife from the kitchen and carefully turned the envelope over. Whitton's name was written on the top. The address was hand-written in block capitals. It was not Smith's address. Smith ran to the kitchen, picked up his mobile phone and dialled Whitton's number.

"Good morning, handsome," Whitton answered it. "Sleep well?"

"Where are you?" Smith asked.

"Just having a cup of coffee with my Dad."

"He knows where you're staying."

"What?"

"The venom psychopath," Smith told her. "There was an envelope on the mat when I got up. It's got your parent's address on the front."

"Oh my God. What do you want me to do?"

"I don't know," Smith tried to think quickly. "Stay there. I'm on my way."

It was Saturday and the roads were quieter than they were during the week but Smith still had to wait in queues of traffic as he made his way to Whitton's parents' house. He parked outside and ran up the driveway. He didn't knock on the door like he usually did. Whitton was in the kitchen with her Mum and Dad. Laura was sitting in her high chair eating breakfast.

"What was in the envelope?" Whitton asked.

"I didn't risk finding out," Smith told her. "I'll drop it off with forensics and get Webber to go over it."

"What does this maniac want?" Harold asked him.

"I really don't know. I have no idea why he's doing this."

"We'd better get to work," Whitton said.

"We'll drive together," Smith said and turned to Harold. "Lock the doors behind us. And don't open anything that comes through the letterbox. I'll see if I can arrange uniform to come and park outside just to be safe."

"I don't think that will be necessary," Harold said. "I'm quite capable of looking after myself and mine."

"Dad," Whitton said. "This is serious. I think you should listen to him."

"No. I'm not about to waste the police's time when there are criminals out there."

"OK," Smith said. "But phone either of us if you notice anything suspicious. Anything."

"Your Dad's a stubborn old bugger isn't he?" Smith said to Whitton as they drove. "I can see where you get it from."

"That's a bit rich coming from you."

"Are you coming in?" Smith asked outside the new forensics building.

"I'll wait in the car," Whitton replied.

"No. I'm not letting you out of my sight."

"My hero," Whitton said and followed him towards the entrance.

Grant Webber was in his office. He grunted a hello when Smith and Whitton came in. Webber was not known to be much of a morning person.

"I need you to have a look at something," Smith told him.

"Of course you do," Webber said. "And don't tell me, it's urgent."

"Extremely." Smith placed the envelope his desk. "Be very careful. I think it came from the venom killer."

Webber was suddenly interested. "I'll get onto it right away."

As they made their way towards the car, Smith remembered something. He needed to check and see if Dr Marx had managed to get hold of any Taipan anti-venom.

"Dr Marx," she answered.

"It's DS Smith. Did you get that anti-venom we spoke about?"

"Not yet. I'm busy at Matthew McLean's house at the moment. Myself and Greg are moving his snakes to the Clifton centre. We can't leave them in the basement."

"I need that anti-venom," Smith said and rang off.

"Anti venom?" Whitton said.

"If somebody is going to be injected with Taipan venom I want to be prepared. The poison from that snake has been known to kill a full grown man in under an hour."

"Why is it that everything that moves in Australia can kill you?" Whitton said.

"They make em tough in Oz."

Bridge and Yang Chu were already there when Smith and Whitton came in. They were drinking coffee in the canteen. Both of them looked exhausted – the past week had taken its toll on all of them.

"The DI's going to be late," Bridge said. "Car trouble. I don't know why she doesn't get a new car. That old Citroen is a real rust-bucket."

"What's the plan, Sarge?" Yang Chu asked.

"I don't have one," Smith admitted. "Keep plugging away until something jumps out at us."

"Same as usual then?" Bridge sighed.

"Right," Smith said. "Let's just re-cap. We'll do this the old fashioned way. Yang Chu, get me a pen and something to write on."

Yang Chu left the room and returned with a notepad and a pen. Smith started writing.

"Frank Broadbent," he wrote. "Killed with venom from a Black Mamba. Young Mark Russell. What was that snake again?"

"Gaboon Viper, Sarge," Yang Chu reminded him.

Smith wrote it down.

"Lisa Sweeney," he continued. "Russell's Viper. And then there was the Krait that killed the man yesterday."

"Anthony Wood," Bridge said.

"You're forgetting Matthew McLean," Whitton joined in.

"Matthew McLean," Smith wrote his name down, followed by the name of the snake that killed him.

"Death Adder," he read what he'd written and something suddenly occurred to him.

Something will jump out at you, lad, Whitton's Dad had said. *Don't try and force it.*

"Fuck," Smith said and ran out of the room.

CHAPTER FIFTY

Smith ran inside the Clifton snake centre. He'd just come from Matt McLean's house – it was locked up and there was nobody inside. Dr Lillian Marx wasn't there like she said she'd be. The man with the long hair smiled when Smith approached.

"You can't keep away, can you? Dr Marx isn't here. She's collecting the snakes from the dead guy's house."

"She's not there," Smith told him. "I've just come from there, and she's not answering her phone either."

"That's odd. Her and Greg left a while ago. They ought to be there by now."

"Greg's the man of few words?"

"He does talk," the receptionist said. "But usually only to people he knows well. He's embarrassed about his voice."

"What's wrong with his voice?"

"Half his tongue is missing, so he speaks with a pronounced lisp."

Everything became clear at the same time. The picture was no longer blurred. It all made sense.

"I need the addresses of both Dr Marx and Greg with the lisp," Smith told the receptionist.

The man wrote them down on a piece of paper and handed it to Smith.

"What's going on?"

"I want you to do something for me," Smith said.

"OK?"

"If Dr Marx and this Greg man come back I want you to phone me on this number." He handed him one of his cards. "And don't tell either of them about it. Is that clear?"

"Clear as day."

He watched with his mouth wide open as Smith ran out of the door.

Smith sat in his car, took out his phone and called Whitton.

"Where are you?" she asked.

"At the snake centre. I think I've figured it all out."

"I thought as much from your dramatic exit earlier."

"It's something Dr Marx said to me yesterday," Smith said. "We were talking about Matt McLean, and she said how awful it must have been to be bitten by a death adder."

"What about it?"

"How did she know he'd been bitten by a Death Adder? Matt had only been dead a few hours and nobody apart from our team knew what snake had bitten him. There was no way Dr Marx could have known unless…"

"Oh my God."

"There's more," Smith said. "The man who she works with at the snake centre hasn't said a word to me each time I've been there, and now I know why. He has a pronounced lisp. I think he's our venom killer and Dr Marx has been helping him all along. I've got both their addresses. I want you and Bridge to go to Dr Marx's house and Yang Chu can meet me at the house of our killer."

He read out both addresses and rang off.

The traffic had thinned out slightly as Smith drove to the address the receptionist had given him for the man with the lisp. Everything now made sense. Not only did the killer have an ingenious method of killing – carrying out the murders without having to be at the scene, he also had an accomplice who was privy to inside information. Smith had to admit it was brilliant.

He parked a few doors down from the house. There was a black hatchback parked outside it and Smith experienced a warming sensation in his stomach. It was the sensation he often felt when he realised they were almost at the end of an investigation. The pieces of the puzzle had been correctly placed together and the picture was almost complete.

"Where the hell is Yang Chu?" he cursed out loud.

He waited a few more minutes then got out of the car and walked up to the house. He couldn't wait any longer. He walked up to the front door and rang the doorbell. It was answered shortly afterwards by Greg, the volunteer from the snake centre.

"Can I have a word?" Smith said. "Greg isn't it? Or is it Boris Boronov?"

"You'd better come in."

Smith knew instinctively he ought to wait for backup, but looking at expression on the face of the man in front of him he reasoned he wouldn't cause too much trouble. He appeared to be almost relieved.

Smith went inside and the man closed the door behind them.

"I'm going to take you in," Smith said. "But first I want to ask you a question. Why?"

"That's a good question," he said in a voice that made Smith's whole body freeze.

It was a voice he'd heard many times before.

"Come through," he gestured for Smith to follow him into the living room. Smith followed him inside, the man with the lisp put his hands in his pocket and with amazing speed he took out a syringe and plunged it into Smith's arm. Smith didn't have time to react.

Whatever he'd been injected with went to work straight away. Smith's vision blurred and his arms became numb. The numbness spread through his chest and down to his legs, everything went black and Smith collapsed in a heap on the carpet.

CHAPTER FIFTY ONE

When Smith woke up he couldn't move. His arms were tied behind his back. He legs were also bound together. He opened his eyes and winced at the bright light. His head was pounding and his mouth felt incredibly dry. He experienced a sudden feeling of déjà vu – he had definitely felt like this before.

"Welcome back," a voice was heard from somewhere in the room. "Did you think it was venom?"

Smith wet his lips with his tongue. "Who the hell are you?"

"You know who I am. Ketamine – that's what I gave you. Nasty stuff. You only had a small dose, but it was enough. You may feel a bit drowsy for a few days and I'd refrain from driving and operating heavy machinery if I were you."

He started to laugh.

"Why are you doing this?" Smith asked.

"Two questions each with the same answer. Who am I? I am Boris Boronov. Why am I doing this? I am Boris Boronov."

He opened his mouth and a forked tongue darted out.

"You knew my father," he continued. "You probably knew him better than I did."

"Viktor Boronov was your father?"

"And you killed him."

Boris Boronov left the room. Smith wriggled his hands behind his back. They had been tied with thin rope and the knot used wasn't a very good one. He managed to loosen it slightly and slip one hand out. He quickly untied the rope binding his legs together but he left the rope there to make it look like he was still tied up. He could hear footsteps so he put his hands behind his back again. Boris came in. He was holding something in his hand that instantly cured his Ketamine hangover. It was a brown snake with a small head. Smith had done enough research in the past week to realise he was looking at a Coastal Taipan. Boris Boronov kissed the serpent on the top of the head.

"Beautiful isn't she? My father is dead because of you, and now it's your turn."

"Your father tried to kill me many times," Smith corrected him. "Your father was pure evil."

"And the apple doesn't fall far from the tree does it? Do you know what one of these can do to you?"

Smith didn't think the question warranted an answer.

"What the hell did Matt Mclean have to do with all of this?" he said.

"Matthew was my channel. My way in."

"You didn't need to kill him."

"Probably not. But, then again, why not?"

"And Dr Lillian Marx?" Smith was still trying to figure it all out, and the Ketamine wasn't helping.

"Everybody has a weak spot," Boris smiled at Smith. "And Lillian's is snakes. She loved snakes."

Smith realised straight away that Dr Marx was dead.

Where the hell is Yang Chu? He thought. *He should have been here by now.*

Boris Boronov held the Taipan's face in front of Smith's.

"You know you're not going to get away with this," Smith said and realised how ridiculous he sounded. "My colleagues are on their way here right now."

"I've already got away with it," he said and laughed again.

Smith tried to formulate a plan in his head. His mind was foggy from the sedative, and the snake Boris Boronov held didn't make it any easier to think straight.

The doorbell rang.

About bloody time, Smith thought. *Yang Chu has arrived.*

"Let's ignore it, shall we?" he spoke to the Taipan then turned to Smith and stuck out the hideous forked-tongue again. "She's beautiful – the Coastal Taipan, but she doesn't have the finesse of her Inland cousin."

He moved his face up to Smith's and his tongue came out again. It was so close it almost brushed against Smith's cheek.

"Now the Inland Taipan isn't as vicious as this lady, but it makes up for that in what's hidden in its venom glands."

The doorbell rang again.

Just open the bloody door, Yang Chu.

"The Inland Taipan," Boris Boronov continued. "Can deliver enough venom to kill a hundred men."

Smith looked at the snake. He needed to somehow get away from the snake.

"Think about that," Boris said. "One hundred men. And right about now there will be an Inland Taipan slithering around inside number 45 Jade Street. Lillian is going to slide her through the letterbox."

It was the address of Whitton's parents.

All Smith could think about was Laura and it spurred him on. It made the deadly snake in front of him disappear.

He lunged for the Taipan and gripped it just under the head. Boris Boronov's eyes widened and his mouth opened. Smith yanked the snake out of his grip and managed to get to his feet. His vision went black for a few seconds then everything became clear again. He thrust the snake's head into Boris Boronov's face, its jaws opened and it attached itself to his nose.

Smith heard the front door open and Yang Chu burst in the room. Smith was still holding on to the Taipan which hadn't released its grip on Boris Boronov's nose. He began to laugh. Yang Chu grabbed him from behind, yanked his hands behind his back and attached a pair of handcuffs. Smith didn't know what to do with the snake. He couldn't let go in case it turned around and bit him. Boris Boronov was still laughing, even with the jaws of a deadly snake attached to his nose.

"What took you so long?" Smith asked Yang Chu.

"Flat tyre," Yang Chu told him. "And the tyre in the boot was also flat. There was a big fight in the city centre so uniform couldn't help. I came in a taxi. Why are you holding onto a snake?"

Smith pulled the Taipan's head away from Boris Boronov's face and frowned. There were no puncture wounds on his nose.

"The lady in your hands is really quite harmless," he told Smith. "No fangs. They were removed after I milked her for the last time. It's sad to see, but her venom has gone to a good home. What do you think one with teeth can do to a baby girl, Jason?"

Smith moved his arm back and swung a punch at Boris Boronov's face with such force that his head was knocked backwards. There was a sickening crunch and blood started to spurt out of his nose. He was about to hit him again when Yang Chu grabbed his arm.

"That's enough, Sarge. He's not worth it."

"Laura!" Smith exclaimed. "We need to get to Whitton's parents' house right away."

Yang Chu took out his phone and called the station.

"It will be quick," Boris Boronov wasn't quite done yet. "But it will be agonising. Are you sure you want to witness that?"

Smith wasn't listening anymore.

"There's an emergency team on the way to Whitton's parents' house," Yang Chu told him. "An ambulance has also been put on standby just in case."

"We need anti-venom," Smith said. "You take care of this sack of shit and I'll go and see if I can find some."

"It won't help," the man on the floor told him.

Smith ignored him. He searched the ground floor and found what he was looking for in a dark room at the end of the hallway. Tanks of snakes were lined up against the wall, and a small refrigerator stood at the back of the room. It was almost a mirror image of Matthew McLean's basement. Inside the fridge were row upon row of various anti-venom. There were sixteen vials of Taipan anti-venom. Smith put all of them in his pocket. He grabbed a couple of syringes and closed the fridge.

CHAPTER FIFTY TWO

Smith jumped out of his car and ran up the drive to Whitton's Mum and Dad's house. He opened the door and went inside. Harold Whitton was lying on his back in the hallway. Whitton and her mother were standing over him. They were both crying. Harold was sweating profusely and his face was deathly pale. There was a copper-brown snake lying by the safety gate at the bottom of the stairs.

"What happened?" Smith asked.

"Laura was sitting on the carpet," Whitton wiped her eyes. "My Dad came to check on her and that's when he spotted the snake. Laura was about to pick it up but my Dad got there first."

"Did it bite him?" Smith asked.

"It just scratched the skin," Harold rasped.

"That's enough to get the venom into your system."

He took out the vials of anti-venom and the syringes, and injected every last one into Harold Whitton's arm.

"Don't fret, lad," Harold said. "It'll take more than a bloody reptile to do me in."

His wife didn't scold him for swearing this time.

   "There's an ambulance on the way," Smith said. "What happened at Dr Marx's house."

"She's dead," Whitton said. "It looks like she was bitten by one of her snakes. She was dead when we got there."

"Poetic justice. Boris Boronov has been arrested. I broke his nose."

"Good on you, son," Harold said and tried to sit up.

"Please don't move," Smith said. "Where's Laura?"

Right on cue Laura came toddling down the hallway. She was holding something in her hand. It looked like a white A4 envelope.

Smith recalled Boris Boronov's words.

Her venom has gone to a good home.

Laura was holding the envelope up in the air. She was tugging at the top.

"Laura," Smith screamed.

If what she was holding was what he thought it was, he had no anti-venom left. He had used every last drop on Harold Whitton.

Laura had her tiny finger under the flap. Smith ran up to her, yanked the envelope out of her hands and threw it against the wall. There was a whistling sound, a tiny needle shot out and the envelope fell to the ground. Smith scooped his daughter up in his arms and kissed her on the top of the head. He left his face their and breathed in her scent.

"Where did the envelope come from?" he asked Whitton.

"It must have been delivered the same time as the snake," her father answered for her. "I didn't even know she'd picked it up."

Two paramedics came in.

"He's been bitten by an Inland Taipan," Smith told them. "I've given him sixteen vials of anti-venom, but he needs to be checked over."

"I'm fine," Harold insisted. "A couple of beers and I'll be right as rain."

Harold Whitton was going to be just fine.

Smith and Whitton rode with him in the ambulance. The anti-venom appeared to be working – his face had regained some of its colour and he wasn't finding it quite so difficult to breathe.

"I have to ask you something," Smith said to him. "What happened to the snake?"

"I knocked its lights out. I'm not scared of a bloody reptile."

"You killed it?"

"It was looking at my only granddaughter funny," Harold said. "And I was having none of it. I get a bit over-protective of my girls sometimes."

"You were bitten by the most poisonous snake on the planet, and you killed it because it was looking at Laura in a funny way?"

"Aye. You'd have done the same if you'd seen the look on its ugly mug."

"Probably," Smith agreed. "You're right - I probably would."

THE END

Printed in Great Britain
by Amazon